Jaq Hazell is the author of I Came to Find a Girl (*Best Crime Fiction of 2015, The Telegraph*). Born near Portsmouth to an Irish mother and an English father, she studied textile design at Nottingham Trent and has an MA in Creative Writing from Royal Holloway, University of London. She has worked as a journalist and magazine editor. She lives in London.

Praise for My Life as a Bench

'This book is a stunner … definitely one that will always remain in my top ten' *Being Unique Books*

'A little gem with love, loss, and life within its pages' *Netgalley Review*

'The writing is perfect, the story is fast-paced, and everything flows smoothly to tie up with a beautiful finish' *This is Lit*

'If you're looking for a unique, but bittersweet read - this book is for you!' *Alissa in Wonderland Reviews*

## ALSO BY JAQ HAZELL

*I Came to Find a Girl*

*London Tsunami & Other Stories*

# My Life as a Bench

Jaq Hazell

✪ Nowness Books

First published 2017 by Nowness Books



A CIP catalogue record of this book is available from the British Library.

www.nownessbooks.com

ISBN: 978-0-9957268-1-9

Cover design: www.patrickknowlesdesign.com

For Z & B

# ONE

There's a bench by the river with my name on it: Lauren Bethany Miller, it says. Only, no one calls me that.

It's Ren – that's what it should say. I knew it was wrong as soon as I arrived, having been unloaded from the back of a truck and positioned on some paving stones.

*I'm not stopping here*, I said.

The workmen – one old, one young and both dressed in yellow high-visibility vests – had placed me between a large beech tree and an old grey bench.

*Excuse me*, I said. *Hello.* Weird they couldn't hear because they were right in front of me reading the plaque that had been fixed to the bench.

'Lauren Bethany Miller,' the older one said, as he shook his head, 'only seventeen – same age as my daughter that is.'

'Look, it's got one of them codes that open a website.' The younger workman pointed his phone at the black on metal encryption code and its screen lit up with my name in curly writing, followed by photos of me as a fat baby through to seventeen. And there was music. *Love that song,* You Know I'm No Good *by Amy Winehouse – only it's me, my version.*

'That must be her singing,' the younger workman said.

'She's good,' the older one said, 'pretty as well.'

*It was Maddy who filmed me. She was, like, my number one fan back then. It was Holly's party – my first proper paid gig – and the night I finally got with Gabe. And there I am in a lacy black dress with my hair pinned up and heavy black eyeliner. I look all right, better than I realised… I want to go back – right there, right then.*

The film cuts to Mum. She's all dressed up in black with her hair curled. She briefly looks away, takes a deep breath and says, 'Nothing's the same since Ren was taken from us.' She looks into the camera and beyond as if she's seen far more of what there is to know than most people. *Poor Mum.*

'My daughter was amazing,' Mum says. 'I know everyone says that about their children, but Ren really was: lively, funny, talented… She wanted to be a singer and she'd have made it given half a chance. She was adorable and loving, and though we sometimes argued, she was my best friend. Losing Ren has left a massive hole in our family that can never be filled, and though I'm grateful for the time we had together, it's so hard. I think of her every minute of every…'

The older workman turned away. 'I can't watch this.'

'You getting emotional?' The younger guy said.

'Leave it out.'

'You are – look at you.'

'Seventeen – that's tragic.'

'What d'you reckon, suicide or drugs?'

'I'd rather not know. Let's finish up and get out of here.'

*I agree*, I said. *The last thing I want is to be reminded of all that.*

They unloaded some machinery and I could see their tattoos. The older guy had an old-school swallow on his hand, while the younger one had a large black snake encircling his arm. *Love tattoos. I've got one. Mum was so angry when she found out. She said it would look terrible when I get old and that I'd go right off it. Well, I never did.*

They placed a large drill on the ground beside me.

*What's that for?* I asked.

The young man shuddered. 'I just had this weird shivery feeling come over me. This bench creeps me out.'

'It's *a bench*,' the other guy said.

'How come you're in such a hurry to finish then? That's not like you.'

'You know how it is, things to do, people to see. Come on, let's get on with it.' The older man went back to the truck that he'd parked up between the bench and the river.

*Excuse me*, I said. *I'm not stopping here. It's boring.*

The older guy passed something to his colleague. 'Here,' he said, 'you do the bending down – save my knees.'

*This isn't funny*, I said. *I don't like it here. I want to go.*

The younger man crouched down and placed a bracket by one of the bench's four legs.

*What's that for?* I said. *What are you doing?*

'Got it?' The older man took out a heavy metal bolt and placed it against a hole in the bracket and drilled.

The sound was deafening and the vibrations caused pins and needles everywhere and cramping. *Stop. I can't stand it.*

They did stop, only they then moved on to the next leg and fixed that with a bolt and bracket as heavy as the first.

*No*, I said. *I don't want this.*

Heads down, they continued.

*Why are you ignoring me?*

They moved on to the third leg.

*No, no more. Stop. It's unbearable. I hate this.*

They worked together without a break, although the older man did stand upright and stretch between fixing each leg.

*You have to stop. This is hell, it really is. I don't want to be here.*

'One more,' the younger man said.

It was brutal that drilling sound, metal on metal.

Once fixed, they stood at either end and shook me.

I was as sturdy as the beech tree next to me.

'That's it, job done,' the older man said.

The younger one nodded. 'This bench ain't going nowhere.'

*No, I don't want this,* I said, expecting them to respond.

Instead, they loaded the equipment back onto the truck and started the engine.

The noise went right through me.

And they were gone.

*I don't get it, they didn't listen. How could they ignore me? I really hate that. Now what?*

I took it all in: the old grey bench to the left, and the large beech tree to the right while ahead there were reeds and the River Thames. And across the river – weeping willows. Beautiful, if you like that sort of thing.

I can't stay here, I thought as I stared at the water, imagining the river rise and overflow, flooding the path with my tears.

Thing is, I know this spot. The bench is about a mile from my dad's house: there's a restaurant in one direction and in the other a café built underneath one of the arches of the bridge. There are loads of benches along this stretch of riverside. Gabe tried to jump them once going from bench to bench. He managed a few but then fell flat on his face and I thought he was hurt and ran over to him, but he just rolled onto his back and pulled me down on top of him, laughing because he'd made me panic.

*Hold on, wait a minute – won't he come? Yeah, 'course he will. He'll sense I'm here, he'll find me. Gabe will come.* I sigh with relief and the cramping subsides. *Gabe, my Gabe, love of my life – and I know that for sure – he will come.*

I watch the bridge, waiting for buses. They're matchbox size and whenever I spot one, I think that must be Gabriel's bus.

*He'll appear on the path beside me any minute, and he'll have that look in his eyes, the one that is only for me. He's bound to be first.*

Forty … fifty … fifty-five, fifty-six buses pass – I count them all day long – and dozens of people, dogs and a few squirrels.

Oh, there's Dad – I think it's him, though it's hard to tell due to the cycling gear: head-to-toe Lycra and a black helmet. He's going slow, cycling up close to the benches, reading what they say. It's him. I recognise that guilty look that flickers across his face whenever he's late.

He looks older, a little hollow around the eyes – not like when I first met him a few months ago.

He's spotted me. There's a faint smile as he dismounts and leans his stupidly expensive bike against the old grey bench next door. He comes around to the front to face me.

*Take that butters helmet off – you look a right neek.*

'Lauren Bethany Miller.' He reads the plaque, and then stands back to get a better look. He nods as if it's the best bench he's ever seen. And then I know – he ordered it. I should have guessed. Only he could be that dumb. *No one calls me Lauren, Dad – why put that? I mean, fair enough, we haven't known each other long, but I was living with you for the last few months. You should know.*

He stares into the distance and his shoulders slump.

*What if my friends can't find me? Even Gabriel might not realise. I hate the thought of him walking past.*

If I had something sharp like a compass or knife, I'd change it right now:

REN WOZ ERE
IS ERE
STUCK
FOREVER
AS IT TURNS OUT

*Why dump me here? It's where the old people sit. Bet that was you too, Dad – it's your sort of place with trees and ducks and the river and stuff, but it's hardly jokes. Where's the buzz? I'd rather be in town by the shops or, even better, outside the fried chicken shop. That place is busy 24/7. And more to the point, it's where I first met Gabe.*

If Dad had set me there I'd see Gabe all the time. I'd love that. I'd love to see him again. I'd give anything.

It's weird that Gabe didn't make the funeral. I guess it was too painful. He'll be missing me for sure.

I can see him now: his light hazel eyes with little dark flecks, all watery – like the time we both thought it was all over. It was such a rush when we finally got back together – literally, the happiest moment of my life. But it's the last time I can't stop thinking about – Gabe's eyes wide and desperate. No one would listen and he was so upset. *Are you OK, Gabe? I really need to know.*

Dad shakes his head as if to break from a trance. He points his phone at the code, clicks, and there I am in a series of embarrassing photos starting with me as a fat baby – did he ever see me like that? The photos cut to the video of me in a black lace dress aged seventeen, singing, eyes closed.

Dad turns off his phone and sits down, his breathing heavy as he stares across the river towards the weeping willows. He ignores everyone – even though many passers-by look at him. He could be an alien in that helmet.

*Anyway, Dad, enough of the grumpy face, you may as well head home – Susannah will be expecting you. And more to the point, I reckon Gabe will be here soon and we definitely need some time alone.*

Funny, Dad does get up, like he's actually listening to me for once. He shivers, sniffs, rubs his hands and reclaims his bike.

*Bye, Dad, good to see you. Please let Gabe know where I am.*

He looks back once more, his eyes wet.

*He does care.*

My eyes also well up, only they don't really because it's impossible. I stare ahead at the water.

What is real?

Birds are flying, the river flows. Life is here and apparent. Am I part of it? I must be. I'm here, aren't I?

I'm hot, my heartbeat fast. Is it all imagined?

Dad didn't see me or hear me.

Am I less than air?

*Gabe, hurry, come, I need you.*
*We are one and the same.*
*You'll see me. You'll know.*

The light's fading – it must be late afternoon.

It's hard to make out people's faces. I bet Gabe will come when less people are around. He'll be emotional and he's shy about stuff like that.

A man approaches. He's hunched against the cold and wearing a heavy coat. He's too big to be Gabriel and his walk is too rigid.

I keep a constant vigil, aware he might miss me because of the misleading plaque. Every passer-by is potentially Gabe – until they come closer. Even the dog-walkers and people with prams – he could be babysitting or helping out a neighbour. He's kind like that, though he does get paid.

What if I fall asleep and miss him?

I try to rise up, cross the bridge and catch a bus to his place. Only I can't.

Why is that? I know where to go, which bus stop, what bus, and where to get off. I remember it all and yet I can't move. What can I do?

I clench my fists and grind the teeth that sit tight in my jaws, only I don't. What is left of me? Am I only thoughts? I wiggle my toes like they told me to – I'm sure I can – but it's only my mind that races onwards, darker, deeper and alone.

# TWO

The river blurs. The lamps have lit, although they're a little way off leaving me in what from a distance must look like total darkness.

I hate the dark. *How will I sleep? Do I sleep? What is this state that I find myself in?* I feel tears welling up and I want to rub my eyes. I can't let myself cry. I won't be able to stop. Again, I see the river rise and imagine my tears flooding the path.

Quick, think of something nice, something good: *Gabriel,* the first time I saw him. Memories are what I have. There he is. I see him, separate, though not alone. No one forgets a look like that.

I go further back to Bourne's. It's my first day – I'm in the common room, a long narrow room built from painted breeze blocks, with Holly Appleby, the blonde with Hollywood teeth who's been assigned to show me around. She's done her duty and introduced me to so many people that I can't remember a single person's name. We sit by the door, but she's fidgety. 'I've got to go meet someone,' she says, 'you'll be OK, yeah?'

'Sure.' I look around at the various groups. Everyone seems close – too close to have room for anyone new. *What if no one speaks to me for the rest of the day? I am screwed. This is what you get for walking out on your life so far. Mum was right.* 'Too impulsive,' she'd said, once she'd found out I'd gone to London to find my dad. I check my phone even though I know there's nothing new. *Text Kemi – look busy.*

'Her boyfriend's an idiot,' says a girl sitting opposite. Is she talking to me? She has a wide face, long dark hair and a steady gaze, and I so want and need to talk to her or someone – anyone…

'You mean Holly?' I ask.

She nods. 'Her boyfriend thinks he's some kind of gangster but he's just a spoilt rich kid. And he puts it about.'

*'I hate that.'*

'You sound like you're talking from experience?'

'I just finished with someone.' I feel myself redden and am instantly too hot. I unzip my hoodie in an attempt to hold it together.

'He messed you about?'

'He won't do it again – no one will.'

'Yeah?' She arches an eyebrow.

'I don't talk to him. I just left.'

'Left where?'

'Devon – that's where I used to live. I moved here a few weeks back.'

She shrugs. 'It's good you dumped him. I mean, I can't stand girls that forgive everything – forget that. If a guy mugs you off, dump him.'

'I agree,' I say, aware I'm nodding too much.

'You here for good?'

'Yeah, definitely,' I say, even though I have no idea if I can stay or not.

'I'm Maddy, by the way.'

'Ren.' I say, almost tearful like she's saved me in some way.

A slim, wavy-haired, blonde girl in a crop top and skinny jeans comes in and says, 'Chicken Shack time, let's go.'

'This is Carina,' Maddy says, 'she's on the fried chicken diet.'

'You look good on it,' I say, thinking she must be one of those lucky girls who can eat anything.

'The food at Chicken Shack is way better than the canteen – trust me.'

Maddy smiles, showing big chunky teeth. 'So it's got nothing to do with a certain person who works there then?'

'There is, like, the fittest dude who serves behind the counter, but shotgun, he's mine – we're getting married, innit.'

'In your dreams,' Maddy says.

'Buy a hat, seriously, it's on,' Carina says. 'Anyway, come on, let's go.'

Maddy pulls on a black jacket, and again I glance around at the various cliques and grip my phone like it holds all the answers. Maddy hoists her bag onto her shoulder. 'You wanna come?' she says, and perhaps it's an afterthought but whatever, I nod and stifle a sigh of relief as my phone slips from my sweaty hand.

Chicken Shack is a small fast food outlet a couple of streets from the college. Its sign is turquoise with a love heart between the words "Chicken" and "Shack".

'Watch her flick her hair and push her chest out,' Maddy says, as Carina pushes the door, flicks her hair and pushes her chest out. And we go straight to the counter, where Maddy nudges me and says, 'That's Idris – the one she loves.'

Carina does a panicked 'Shush' and Idris turns around and smiles.

'He likes you,' I say.

'She'll stalk him, whatever,' Maddy says. 'He doesn't stand a chance.'

We sit on the left-hand side with our boxes of chicken and fries set out on the plastic table. Carina spends most of the time flicking her hair and glancing at Idris, until a group of lads walk in and a look passes between her and Maddy. At the most opportune moment, they turn and say, 'All right.'

'All right,' the first lad says, while the second nods and the third grunts as they make their way to the counter. The last one, the one with light hazel eyes and high cheekbones, looks over and catches my eye for what must be only a matter of seconds but feels way longer. I look away. It's intense, too much almost, and yet I look back as does he and I have to look away again.

I put down my food. *He's the best-looking boy I have ever seen.*

And for that moment my ex Griff is all but forgotten. Nothing can ever be the same again – somehow I know. I glance back again, I can't help it – he is so beautiful, with the sort of face you can't believe is possible. I have to know who he is. Something's started, I know it for sure – I like him, he likes me, how hard can it be?

I watch him at the counter. He studies the menu and whispers to his nearest friend, who turns and looks back at me, while I lean in towards Maddy so as not to be overheard. 'Who are they?' I ask.

'You don't waste any time,' she says.

I shrug. 'I'm just curious – thought I might know them.'

Maddy does that arched eyebrow thing she does and says, 'Yeah, right, you've only just moved here.'

'They go to Cam's,' Carina says.

'Cam's?'

'College down the road.'

'Is that like a proper sixth-form college?'

'Are you saying Bourne's ain't a proper college?' Maddy says.

'You know what I mean – Bourne's is a school with a sixth form.'

'Cam's is a proper college,' Carina says. 'I wanted to go there, but my mum thinks Bourne's is the best school around here. As if.' She rolls her eyes.

I feel sick to my stomach, instinctively sure that I should have gone there. But then that's what you get when you walk out of your college/family/life-so-far and turn up on your estranged dad's doorstep unannounced. They said I could only stay if I agreed to go to college in London, and then they dumped me in Bourne's – the only college with a vacancy within a ten-mile radius. I'd rather have gone to Cam's. Imagine that, I could have been at college with the most beautiful boy I've ever seen.

'So, you know those guys right?' I ask again.

'The first guy's Aaron,' Carina says, 'he thinks he's way hotter than he is.'

Maddy interrupts. 'She wants to know about Gabriel.'

Carina gives a knowing look. 'Everyone thinks he's cute, don't they, Maddy?'

'He's in a thing with someone,' Maddy says.

'I didn't know that,' Carina says. 'Who's he seeing?'

'Georgia Hills. She's at Cam's.'

I look down at my drink to hide my disappointment.

It's over before it's begun, another untrustworthy idiot. I hate that kind of thing, so really he's the last person I want to see on the bus home.

It's packed, standing room only, and he's at the back with his mates, including a loud one who waves and blows kisses. I'm by the exit, squashed up in the space for a wheelchair. My phone goes off. It's Mum. I turn it off and stare ahead.

Gabriel moves down the bus towards me and our eyes meet again, only this time I think, why look at me when you're already 'in a thing' with someone else?

Gabriel nods and smiles with a warm look that lingers as long as possible before he leaps from the bus and gives his mates the finger as they jeer out the window. They're all the same, I think, whether it's London, Devon or wherever. But, even so, the warmth of his gaze did something to me.

The night is long – long enough to relive everything: how we first talk, what he says, and how we link up on Facebook. Finally, we're together and there's the first kiss, the parties, the days out in Camden and how we escape everyone else and go where we shouldn't. I love him, he loves me, I love everything about him, and he's beautiful and exciting and fun to be with. I'm the luckiest girl.

The night is long, too long. It's as if it lasts forever as I relive it all. Again we break up and I don't get why, which makes it even worse and there's that grinding pain that will never end. And it really doesn't, not until we make up that is, when it dissolves away to reveal literally the happiest moment in my life as Gabriel holds my face and looks so lovingly – his hazel eyes concentrated wholly on me. Some people never get a look like that. It's for real.

Ren and Gabe forever.

The night is long. It lasts forever. The days will too if Gabriel doesn't come.

*I miss you, Gabe. Please hurry.*

The blackness surrounds me. I can't sleep.

*Will I relive everything? Tell me I won't – not again.*

But it comes. It's here. I can't avoid it.

Disaster strikes all over again, and even though I know what to expect, it still catches me out as it arrives seemingly from nowhere to play out in slow motion like there's beauty even in the bad.

And then comes the screaming.

*Make it stop.*

*Please make it stop.*

It stops only as the darkness lifts. And the sunrise glows pink behind the clouds – one of those things you're supposed to appreciate, but without Gabriel it's nothing.

# THREE

You're over the worst.

*Who said that?*

The first night is particularly hard.

*What? Excuse me, is that you – the old grey bench next door?*

Yes, my dear.

*You mean I'm not the only one stuck here?*

That is correct.

*You're freaking me out.*

I apologise if that is the case.

*Who are you?*

My name is Lionel – and you are Lauren, I believe?

*It's Ren – I prefer Ren – that's what my friends call me.*

Welcome to the riverside, Ren.

*Er, thanks, I think. How long have you been here?*

It's hard to say. I do take note of the seasons, but one struggles to keep track of the years. Perhaps you can help?

*It's 2012.*

Are you sure about that?

*I swear it's 2012*, I say, but he gets me thinking: has there been a gap? How can I not be sure?

Your last moments alive – during which season did they occur?

*It was winter, before Christmas*, I say, as I allow myself to think only of Gabriel's beautiful face.

Ah, this is the problem. It is most certainly winter. Do you not agree?

*Well, yeah, the trees are bare, people are wearing heavy coats.*

Therein lies the rub – winter straddles the end of one year and the beginning of the next and so the exact year remains unclear until spring at least.

*Suppose it's 2012 – if that's the case, how long have you been here?*

Let me see, that would make it twenty-two years.

*You've been stuck here twenty-two years?*

It must be something like that, yes – give or take a few months, I suppose.

*And you say I'm over the worst?*

The first night is the longest.

*Every minute feels way too long.*

You're waiting for someone, he says.

*How do you know that?*

There's always a reason.

*The bench and plaque were ordered for me – it's not like I had a choice.*

There's someone you have to see?

*Yeah, my boyfriend Gabriel. I'm longing to see him. He's my life.*

Indeed.

*I can't believe it. I thought we had forever.*

It's the mistake we all make.

*But I'm only seventeen – how was I to know?*

The brown river water turns slightly choppy as a breeze stirs the trees.

Two red London buses pass over the bridge. *Gabriel might be on one of them. Please let him be – I'd give anything.* I study the bridge and path – hoping.

A couple of geese land on the water.

A woman with her hair tied back pushes a pram, with a dog on a lead by her side, followed by a sheepdog ahead of its jogging owner, and a man with greased-back grey hair and a dark suit. *No Gabriel.*

The wind carries a leaf across the path.

*Are you still there?* I ask Lionel after a minute or so.

Ha! What remains?

*Sorry?*

What remains? That is the question.

*I don't get what you mean.*

Never mind. One has too much time to think, that is all.

*How old are you, or rather were you when…?*

When I passed?

*Yeah, I mean I don't want to upset you or anything it's just…*

You're curious.

*Yeah.*

Trombones.

*Trombones?*

Don't you know the song – *Seventy-Six Trombones*?

*No, never heard of it. But I take it you're seventy-six then?*

I was at the point of expiration, yes.

*Does that make you seventy-six or are you like seventy-six plus twenty-two, which is, let me see – ninety-eight?*

I assume my age is fixed at seventy-six rather than ninety-eight, but one cannot be sure.

*Well, you're well old either way.*

Thank you for that. You're from around here, I presume?

*My dad is. I'm from Devon.*

A Devonshire lass? Well, I never – whereabouts?

*I doubt you've heard of it: Bovey Tracey – it's near Newton Abbot.*

I've been to Newton Abbot on my way to Dartmoor – must be about fifty years ago now. I climbed Haytor with my daughter.

*I've been up Haytor a million times. We even had to go with the school.*

It's a stunning view, Lionel says. Quite a climb as I remember – it would be an interesting spot for a bench.

*Nah, it would be boring as – worse than here.*

You don't like it here?

*I'd prefer somewhere buzzier, with a bit of life.*

One can't live vicariously, you know.

*What can I do? Is there anything?*

It's not for me to say. One has to find one's own way in death as in life.

I take a deep imaginary breath to steady myself, alarmed and upset by my obvious limitations. Lionel, this bench next to me, knows everything I need to know and I suspect none of it will please me.

The sky darkens with the threat of rain.

*Are you from London?* I ask.

Born and bred.

*Lucky, I love London.*

There is luck involved in such matters and one is grateful to have been born a Londoner, although it was rather trying during the war.

*Better than Devon, whatever.*

How have you ended up here by Old Father Thames?

*It's my dad. He ordered it – the bench, I mean.*

He lives nearby?

*Yeah, I was staying with him the last few months.*

Ah, I see. What were you doing in London?

*Avoiding Devon mainly, or at least I was at the start.*

Why was that?

*You know, the usual stupid-cheating-boyfriend stuff.*

This chap – Gabriel, was it? He cheated on you?

*No, not Gabriel, it was the one before, Griff.*

A sudden heavy downpour turns the riverside path to the colour of charcoal. A woman opens a red polka-dot umbrella, while another raises a black one. And they increase their pace. Everyone hurries. And I try to remember what it feels like to move, walk, break into a run.

# FOUR

My stepmother Susannah has brought the dogs.

The rain's stopped but the sky remains grey, and like a glamorous Girl Guide, Susannah is prepared for all weathers in a waxed coat, jeans and boots, with her sleek blonde hair peeking out from beneath a hat. 'There's no such thing as bad weather, only the wrong clothing' – that's what she said the first time we met, as she looked me up and down. It was raining heavily, much like today, and yet I was wearing only a hoodie and shorts.

The dogs go straight for me, pissing against the bench.

I swear I hear Lionel laugh.

*Max, George, beat it*, I shout, and they do back off briefly before returning to sniff around the back where George cocks his leg against me again. *Seriously, get lost.*

Susannah checks the bench and its plaque just as my dad did. She removes her leather gloves, leans forward and touches the engraved lettering.

'I'm sorry, Ren,' she says, her mouth set straight.

She points her phone at the code on the plaque and the screen lights up with my name in big curly letters followed by the series of photos from chubster to seventeen and then cuts to me in that black lace dress singing Amy Winehouse at Holly's party.

Susannah perches on the edge of the wet seat as she watches it all: the singing, Mum's eulogy, and the tributes from family and friends. Everyone's there on that video montage of my short life, everyone apart from Gabe… Why is that – was he too upset to be filmed? *Are you OK, Gabe? I wish you'd hurry up and come. There's so much I want to know.*

Susannah stares ahead at the reeds and the weeping willows.

*Is it still 2012?* I ask.

A man cycles past and a lady in heels clip-clops towards the bridge that will take her into town. Susannah stares ahead.

Why won't she answer? There's a lump in my non-existent throat.

The brown river flows and the branches of the weeping willows whip up into frenzied waves as if they're making fun of the fact I can no longer move. Why can't I move? It's so unfair. I want to get up and go find Gabe – let him know.

Susannah places her gloved hands either side of herself and presses down on the seat of the bench.

*Susannah, it's me, Ren. Can you hear me? You know what a great stepmother you are – do me a favour and call Gabe; tell him I'm here waiting for him?*

The dogs bark.

'That's enough, boys.' Susannah stands up.

*Susannah, wait – promise me you'll call Gabe; I beg you call him. I'm dying to see him – well, you know what I mean.*

She looks back at the bench. I think she's frowning, but it's a weird Botox non-frown that makes her forehead look like a breeze-blown puddle.

She turns to go.

*Please,* I shout, *don't forget to call Gabe.*

Again, the dogs bark but Susannah doesn't look back.

Begging won't help, Lionel says.

*Are you here just to piss me off?*

My dear, may I remind you that I am one of the more established members of this riverside community. I have been here for many years before you showed up.

*You're probably making up for lost time – now you've someone to talk to.*

You don't seriously think I've been alone all this time?

*I dunno, I hadn't given it a thought.*

There was someone else before you, you know.

*Who was that?*

Norman.

*Where's he gone?*

They took him away.

*Who did?*

The workmen.

*Why?*

I believe they call it a programme of riverside refurbishment.

*Norman was also a bench?*

Yes, of course.

*How long had he been here?*

He arrived the year before me.

*So, how come you survived the cull?*

Norman didn't wear well.

*How come?*

His wood was of an inferior quality.

*I guess your days are numbered though.*

It's not a concern. Who was the lady with the dogs?

*My stepmother.*

Is she wicked?

I laugh. *I thought so at first.*

Why?

*She didn't want to let me in the house. Although to be fair, she'd never heard of me and I did show up without warning.*

How old were you at the time?

*Seventeen. It was only a few months ago.*

Good heavens, and she knew nothing of your existence?

*It's complicated.*

Go on.

*I don't want to talk about it.*

Lionel sighs. It's been an awfully long time since I heard anything new. Bear in mind they took Norman away in the spring.

*Spring? That was like nearly a year ago.*

Indeed, it was.

*You've been alone that long?*

We are all alone.

*That's cheerful.*

Ah, I take it you can now appreciate why I am so keen to hear about you.

*Yeah, well, fair enough, but don't blame me if you get bored.*

You're anything but boring, my dear.

*It was pissing it down the day I arrived at my dad's house. I'd travelled for nearly four hours on two trains and a bus and then walked the last part only to find myself stuck outside a locked gate, so I rang the buzzer/intercom thingy, but no one answered and I thought, shit, what now?*

You can spare me the language, thank you, Lionel says.

*Sorry, bad habit, can't help it. Anyway, I thought, try again and if no one answers then panic, because I didn't even have enough money for a sandwich, let alone a train back to Devon.*

And someone did answer?

*Yeah, eventually there was this posh female voice. I didn't expect a woman to answer. I don't know what I expected really, but I suppose I sort of imagined my dad would be there waiting for me, which was really stupid because of course he'd be at work at that time.*

*Anyway, the woman got a bit funny with me. 'Hello, can you not hear me?' she said. I asked if Nicholas Miller (that's my dad) was there, and she said he was not.*

*'When's he due back?' I asked, and she said, 'Who is this?' So I told her my name and all she said was, 'What is it you want?', which really threw me because I thought she'd recognise the name. 'What do you want?' she repeated, and I just blurted it out, 'I'm Nicholas Miller's daughter, Lauren. He's my dad.' And there was this long drawn-out crackle from the intercom before she said, 'You'd better come in.' And finally, the electric gate opened revealing this*

*massive white house, big enough to be a small hotel.*

Goodness, your father must be extremely rich.

*Yeah, really, and I had no idea or I'd have looked him up sooner.*

That's a joke, I take it?

*Yeah, course.*

I must say it sounds intriguing. Tell me about this hotel-like mansion?

*It's called Ambrose House. It has four floors and loads of windows. It's old-fashioned, though I'm not sure how old. I'd never been in such a big house and I had butterflies as I approached the front door. But it didn't open at first, and because my mum always says it's rude to stand on the step, I stayed out in the rain like a right lemon. I could hear all this barking, and then the door opened and a dog ran at me. 'George, down,' the woman shouted. She had hold of another dog by its collar. And the dogs were identical, like they'd both just escaped from an Egyptian tomb.*

Ah, the dogs that recently visited. What breed are they?

*Pharaoh hounds. They're hunting dogs – mean-looking, aren't they?*

I hope they didn't hurt you?

*No, she managed to call them off.*

She invited you in?

*Yeah, after she checked my ID, would you believe?*

Well, as a pensioner, I can appreciate the need for caution.

*I thought it was rude, but I showed her my bank card anyway.*

And she invited you in?

*Yeah, though she didn't take me into any of the fanciest rooms.*

Not the tradesmen's entrance, surely?

*What?*

Never mind.

*She told me to take off my shoes, which was embarrassing because my tights were wet and I could see I was leaving footprints. And then she took me down to the basement where there's this huge room, bigger than a village hall – that's the kitchen, and it even has a glass wall through which you can see the swimming pool.*

Next to the kitchen – how bizarre, Lionel says.

*It's a bit of a trend. Loads of rich people dig out their basements. Susannah says some people even have underground ballrooms, art galleries and car parks for all their fast cars. She reckons their kitchen and swimming pool are modest compared to what her friends have.*

She must have some very fine friends.

*Yeah, well, all snobs as far as I could make out.*

Oh dear, is she like that?

*I thought so at first. I mean she wasn't exactly pleased to see me. I remember looking at the pool and going, 'That's sick.' But Susannah made out it was nothing special. She just shrugged and said, 'Alicia likes it'. And I thought, who the hell is Alicia? Turns out she's my sister, though I had to ask. Susannah didn't tell me anything unless I asked.*

Tricky, Lionel says. One always has to know what to ask.

*I kept staring at the pool, longing to dive in, so when Susannah passed me a towel I thought she'd read my mind. But luckily, I asked what the towel was for because she looked me over and said, 'You're wet from the rain, would you not like to dry yourself? I know I'd like to keep a dry floor.'*

Bit of a cold fish? Lionel says.

*What, you mean, like, unfriendly? Yeah, well, she did all the right things – you know, made me a drink and sat me down. But it was awkward. There were too many questions.*

*She asked my age and when I said I was seventeen, she looked at this big clock on the wall like it would help her work out some fundamental calculation. And she kept staring.*

*I knew what she was thinking – does this girl look like Nicholas? Is she really his daughter? Because she then goes, 'I don't get it. I've never heard of you. Why haven't I heard of you? Nicholas doesn't know about you – is that it?'*

*But I wasn't having that. 'He knows,' I said. 'He must do. He pays child maintenance. There was a letter from his solicitors – Clifford & Parkes.'*

*It was like I'd slapped her. She even felt her cheek. And it was then I noticed her ring. What a diamond – it's massive, with loads of little ones dotted around it. She got up, moved away and stood with her back to me, staring at the pool.*

*I offered to go out and come back later, but she said, 'What, in this weather?' and she looked real tense like I'd totally ruined her day. 'Give me a minute,' she said, and left the room.*

*A short older woman with black hair came in and said, 'Hello, I Marie, Susannah ask me to come make you something to eat. What you like?' Susannah didn't want to leave me alone in her house, I reckon.*

*Anyway, what the hell, I didn't want to eat. Instead I asked to use the toilet. Marie told me there was a choice of two on that floor. They have toilets and bathrooms everywhere – it's like the rich must shit more.*

Ren, please, Lionel says, that's extremely crass.

*Soz.*

Soz?

*Sorry.*

What is this language you speak?

*It's how young people speak, innit.*

Innit?

*Isn't it.*

It's different to the slang I remember.

*Multicultural, innit.*

I see.

*Anyway, I went in this piff toilet that's more like the sort of changing rooms you get at a posh health club, and I then made a detour to check out the pool. And that's where Susannah found me. 'Where's she gone?' I heard her say, and before I could get back she spotted me through the glass. 'What are you doing?' Her face looked glazed, but I swear she was trying to frown.*

She can't frown?

*Botox, innit.*

Botox?

*Jeez, it's complicated talking to you. It's not like Doctor Who – when he turns up in another time and dimension he understands everything.*

I've heard of *Doctor Who.*

*You probably saw the first episode.*

Yes, perhaps I did.

*Botox is this chemical that gets injected into the face. It, like, freezes the muscles to stop wrinkles, but I think it makes people look weird like they're too smooth and yet puffy.*

Ah, plastic surgery – now that has been around a while.

*Anyway, I ignored her non-frown frown and walked back through and apologised, explaining that the pool was just so amazing I had to get a closer look. And then she said that she'd spoken to Nicholas (my dad), and that he was on his way. And immediately I felt a bit faint and panicky like it was some kind of warning that I shouldn't have come.*

Ah, no, Lionel says. I fear for you now. There is only one true lesson that life taught me and that is that one should always follow one's instinct.

*Yeah, well, I couldn't really turn around and run back to Devon. It was late and I had no money. And besides, perhaps it was following my instinct that took me there in the first place. I mean as soon as I found out Griff had cheated on me I knew I had to get as far away as possible and to me that meant London to go find my dad.*

*Thinking about it, if I'd never come to London to meet my dad I'd never have met Gabe and if I'd never met Gabe then I wouldn't have truly lived.*

# FIVE

The rain resumes, sudden and torrential with thunder and lightning. People run if they can. It's the afternoon crowd: mums and kids, pensioners returning from the shops and dog walkers. A chocolate Labrador makes a beeline for the front of me where Susannah's dogs had been.

You'll get them all now, Lionel shouts. Once they start, that's it – dog after dog – they love to urinate over the previous dog's markings.

Warm liquid splashes at the bench's front leg.

*That's gross*, I say.

The owner yanks at the dog's lead. 'Enzo, hurry up.'

A cyclist passes: tall and straight-backed with a creaky bike, swiftly followed by a younger woman on a racing bike that soon overtakes. There's a man with a bulging kitbag and another wearing only a shirt, trousers and gloves. *Idiot.*

A plastic bottle bobs on the river.

Another dog arrives to cock its leg at the usual spot.

*Ugh, that's the fifth dog today*, I shout, thinking Lionel won't hear me over the rain. *Seriously, I would have lost the will to live if I wasn't already dead.*

Five dogs and yet no Gabriel – I don't get it.

What if he's met someone else?

No, he can't have done, not without telling me.

Strange he's not here though.

Why doesn't he come?

He doesn't know – that's it.

Tell him, Dad, Susannah, tell Gabe where I am.

And tell him you got my name wrong and that there's some dumb-arse plaque that says "Lauren Bethany Miller" – because I really want to see Gabriel.

# SIX

The night draws in.

Will I relive it all again?

Daylight colours fade to greys while a heavy beat thumps within me. Everything's tight: shoulders, fists and teeth clenched – phantom memories of what it is to feel and be?

Lionel is quiet.

Polite warning, he says, I don't converse beyond dusk.

*Why's that?*

No particular reason, it's purely by choice.

*All right, whatever – goodnight then.*

Goodnight, my dear, rest in peace.

*Is that a joke?* I say, but he doesn't answer. It's like he's put up a "Do Not Disturb" sign leaving me in the dark, longing to be further along the riverside either way where there are lamps glowing warm yellow light that reflects back off the water.

The black branches of the beech tree move like tentacles within a dark sea and all I can do is wish myself away to the moment when I first saw Gabriel.

It's lunchtime and I'm at Chicken Shack with Maddy and Carina on the left-hand side when in walk a group of lads. Maddy and Carina look at one another and turn to say hello. The guys all reply, apart from the last one who looks only at me. And it's like his soft steady gaze goes right into me. Who is he? I watch him at the counter. He glances back and whispers to a friend. 'Who are they?' I ask, but all Maddy and Carina say is that they go to Cam's, the college down the road. *But who are they?* Or, more to the point, *who is he?* Maddy narrows her eyes and tells me he's called Gabriel and that he's "in a thing with someone" and within a matter of minutes I have loved and lost.

Later, I see him on the bus and again his warm soft stare does something to me. Ignore it, I tell myself as I think of my cheating ex. They're all the same.

Back at my dad's place, I key in the code and the wooden gate slowly opens to reveal the mansion that is Ambrose House. It's been two weeks and I'm not used to it. A house that grand has to be a target for burglars. I head downstairs and am relieved to find Marie the housekeeper at the breakfast bar surrounded by glass storage jars that she's filling with gross dried stuff.

'Ah, Ren, you have nice day?'

'It was OK. That looks rank. What you cooking?'

'Susannah ask I make kale, quinoa and black beans.'

'I'll just grab a sandwich, thanks.'

I look towards the glass wall that splits the basement between the kitchen and swimming pool. The perfect blue rectangle glitters under the spotlights. *I should swim – work off that fried chicken.* But instead I make out I have homework and head upstairs to my room, the Hummingbird Suite, named after its hand-painted wallpaper, which is gold with red tubular flowers and hummingbirds.

I bung my rucksack onto the gold bedspread and fall backwards onto the bed to check my phone. There's a message from Kemi (my best friend back home): 'Skype me'.

I fire up my laptop and call her.

She's small and cute with her big brown eyes and apple cheeks squished into her tiny box room that looks even smaller thanks to the wall-to-wall band posters.

'Badgers.' I grin as I say it, and she does the same. It's a thing we've done for years after watching a documentary as kids. Badgers scratch a lot – especially their backsides and we found that funny and started the "Badgers Appreciation Society" where we'd walk around looking for badgers, but never saw any – not alive anyway, and so instead we'd just shout "badgers", which probably scared them off anyway.

'Wow,' Kemi says, 'whenever I see you in that massive room I can't believe it. It's like you've gone to live in a palace.'

'Be all right if it wasn't for the food. Kale and quinoa tonight.'

'What's that?'

'Healthy shit. What's happening down there?' I ask, and Kemi knows what I mean because her face drops making the apple cheeks disappear.

'You're not going to like this.'

'Go on,' I say, even though I know it's going to relate to Griff, my recent ex and the reason I walked out on my college/family/life-so-far.

'Griff's going out with Izzy.'

'Seriously?'

Kemi nods, her face solemn.

'Since when?'

'I think they kept it secret for a while. It's out of order – everyone says so.'

'I'm glad I'm not there right now.'

'Aw, Ren, you're too good for him anyway. He's a dick.'

I wipe my eyes and nod in agreement.

'Did you start your new college?'

'Yeah.' And then I think of Gabriel and how he's in a thing with someone and yet looking at me. 'What is it with guys – why can't they be honest?'

'I know.'

'College is OK, but I miss you.'

'Aw, I really miss you. When can I come and stay?'

'Any time,' I say, like it's my mansion and I can invite whomever I like whenever without even asking. And then I lie and say I've stuff to do, when really all I want is to sit on the floor, lean against the bed and listen to Amy.

And I'm crying of course, because of Griff and Izzy and even a little for Gabriel because he looks so good and yet obviously isn't, as I stare at the wallpaper with its damn hummingbirds that are painted in mating pairs like they're all crazy in love. And I close my eyes and: *It's the one and only Miss Amy Winehouse with Ren Miller, singing* Love Is A Losing Game.

# SEVEN

Susannah's standing in the doorway, and I have no idea how long she's been there.

'Was that you singing?' she says, her hair all puffed out with perfect blonde roots. She must have had it done.

'Are you spying on me?' I'm unhappy she didn't knock.

'It was loud. I could hear you from Alicia's room. It was you, wasn't it?'

*Am I making too much noise now? Is that what she means?*

'Well, was it you or a recording?'

'Yeah, it was me. So?'

'You're really good.'

It's all that pain, I think.

'Has your dad heard you?'

I don't get why she's asking this, especially as they both made such a big deal about me singing the day Mum and Jay turned up to take me home. I'd been there a week – uninvited admittedly, but they'd made me feel pretty welcome. I got up late on the Saturday and went downstairs to the kitchen where Alicia was at the table drawing fashion models in slutty dresses. And Nicholas was leaning over the breakfast bar reading the paper.

'How come you're here?' I asked.

'I do live here and pay all the bills, etc.'

'Yeah, but you're usually out torturing yourself with all that cycling,' I said. Alicia giggled, and the dogs started barking, the doorbell went, and Nicholas shot upstairs.

'Why didn't he use the intercom?'

'I have no clue,' Alicia said.

A moment later it all became clear as Nicholas said, 'You're looking well, Annie,' and I heard Mum's voice, and Jay.

It was strange to see Mum there in Ambrose House. Dressed in boot-cut jeans and a wool jacket, she looked older, frumpier and more middle-aged than I remembered, or perhaps it was the change of environment. She looked all right in our little house in Bovey. I mean, she always made an effort, had her hair highlighted and some of her clothes were OK. But seeing her there in Dad's smart subterranean kitchen, she looked dowdy and out of place.

I went to her and we hugged, and Nicholas introduced first Alicia and then Susannah and I wondered what Mum and Jay would think. Alicia was in her riding gear – jodhpurs and polo shirt – while Susannah was all blonde hair in a tight, high ponytail with her yoga/Pilates-trim, organic-fed body squeezed into skinny jeans and a pink cashmere jumper, as she smiled her perfect teeth-whitened smile, shook hands and offered drinks.

'It's like a footballer's house,' Jay said, and the glass that separates the kitchen from the swimming pool steamed up in front of him so I guess he must have been open-mouthed with amazement.

Mum fixed me with one of her looks. 'Fancy taking off like that – did something happen at college? Was it Griff?'

'I don't want to talk about it.'

'Who's Griff?' Nicholas asked.

'The boyfriend – has she not mentioned him? That's telling.'

'He's not my boyfriend.'

'Actually, she's not said much about her friends at all,' Nicholas said.

'That's odd. Her friends are everything. What's going on?'

'Nothing.'

'Ren, we can't help you unless we know what's happened?'

'Nothing. Stop going on.'

'Still wearing those hideous shorts, I see.' Mum looked down at my cut-off shorts, her forehead squished up in a way Susannah's never could, and I remembered the argument we'd had at breakfast the day I left – over what I was wearing.

'Stop criticising everything. You're so negative.'

Mum took a deep breath and said, 'How long did it take you to get here?'

I thought of the first train and the creep who sat opposite and stared at my crotch until I put a bag on my lap and scowled at him. He got off at the next stop, but even so it did make me question what I was doing. *I mean Griff's an arsehole, but all the way to London – really?*

'It took ages,' I said, 'like half a day.'

Mum nodded. 'I knew it must have taken a while, so I thought we'd come up and collect you – save you the awful journey home.' I felt her stare penetrate my skull as she tried to force her will on me.

'I'm not going back.' Funny, I only decided then, at that moment, like it was a deliberate decision to do the opposite of whatever Mum wanted. Mum had assumed she could simply turn up, have a quick chat and persuade me to return, but I wasn't having it and that meant we all ended up around the table in some deep discussion about my future.

'I've had it with college,' I said, and that set them all off.

Nicholas called for paper and Susannah promptly passed him a notepad and pens like she was his secretary or something and that made me smile – as it did Mum.

He drew two columns, one headed "College", the other "Alternatives".

'I'll start,' he said. 'College and A levels lead to university, improved job prospects, higher earnings and more job satisfaction.'

'Not necessarily,' I said. 'Some jobs you can't study for.'

'Like what?'

I hesitated, and felt myself redden. 'Singing,' I said.

'Singing?' Susannah went boggle-eyed, I swear.

'Yeah, singing.'

'You want to be a singer?' Nicholas said.

'I'd like to be a singer,' Alicia said.

'Shush, Alicia,' Susannah said, 'this is serious.'

'Ren *can* sing,' Mum said.

'You can't get her off the karaoke,' Jay said.

'She's good,' Mum said, 'and I do encourage her to follow her dreams, but she needs a back-up plan.'

'That's like preparing to fail,' I said.

'The music business is notoriously fickle,' Nicholas said. 'I strongly recommend you do acquire some qualifications in case the singing doesn't work out.'

'You've got to get out there while you're young though,' I said.

'Yeah, but you've got to look the part in the first place, which might be a problem for Ren.' Jay laughed, and I punched his upper arm.

'Do you play any instruments?' Susannah asked.

'Guitar – a bit.'

'You have lessons?'

'I taught myself. I prefer doing things on my own.'

'Do you write your own songs?'

Again, I felt myself redden. 'I'm not very good – not yet, anyhow.'

'I'd like to hear you sing.' Susannah sat back in her chair, her eyes narrowed.

'What, like now?' I looked at them all seated around the long wooden table. 'This is awkward.' I couldn't do it, however much they all went on, it just made me want to run from the room and never go back. 'Stop going on at me – you're all making me feel rubbish, like you think I can't do it.'

And it went on like that, escalating to a full-blown argument. I was adamant I wouldn't go back to college in Devon and so the adults agreed I'd have to enrol at a college in London, whether I liked it or not.

And so here I am after my first day, and Susannah's finally heard me sing after eavesdropping at the door of my room.

'Nicholas really must hear you sing.'

I shrug. I mean it's not like my dad's around much – when will he hear?

Alicia comes in, dressed in her school uniform – a long burgundy tartan skirt and grey jumper – butters.

'I told you to get changed,' Susannah says.

Alicia replies in what I assume is Mandarin.

'What does that mean?' Susannah asks.

Alicia turns to me. 'I said, "Your singing's a delight".'

'Is that for real? Because I'm going to check on Google Translate and there'll be trouble if you said I've got a fat arse.'

'I said that too.' Alicia laughs and flops onto one of the armchairs.

'Make yourself at home.'

Susannah perches on the other chair. 'So, how did it go?' she says.

'What?'

'College, of course. It *was* your first day.'

'Oh yeah, well, the food's terrible and there's, like, loads of stupid rules about what you can and can't wear, but the people seem all right.'

'Not too bad then?'

'I guess.'

'Well, let's see how it goes. There are private options. You're still on the waiting lists. We can always move you later if it doesn't work out. Right, it's suppertime. I want you both downstairs in five.'

'I ate at college.'

'What did you have?'

I think of Chicken Shack and the box of fried chicken. She'd think it was evil, like it was the food of the devil. Susannah is studying for a post-grad in nutrition and is health-obsessed. So I lie, and say, 'I had a pasta pot with cheese.'

'Did they not have anything healthier?'

'Pizza.'

'Is that all?'

'Sausage rolls.'

'I suggest you take a packed lunch tomorrow. I'll ask Marie to make up some salad. Right, you can still come and sit with us while we eat. We always have meals together. Downstairs in five.'

*Can you call kale and quinoa a meal?*

I open Facebook and click on Griff (my ex): "In a relationship with Izzy Bowles", it says, and there are photos: him with a fag in his mouth (bad man) while Izzy simpers beside him in a vest top looking all gooey-eyed and pathetic. *Bitch.* I click through to her page and it's totally Griff with photos of her and him on loads of different dates. My stomach lurches. How long has this been going on? *I am so stupid.* I bury my head in a pillow.

And I lie like that, face down, and think of Bourne's and all the new people I met today, but I don't know anyone's full name apart from Holly Appleby – the girl who was supposed to show me around and look after me but slipped out to meet her boyfriend, making me a sad loner.

I jump up and click onto her Facebook page. There she is, looking slim and golden, and that must be her boyfriend with the platinum-blonde hair. He's making out his fingers are a gun and pointing them towards the camera. *Idiot.* She has 1,007 "friends". I scroll through the photos. There he is, that's him, the one I like (or rather liked until I heard he was unavailable). He's called Gabriel Walker. I click through to his profile page expecting to see photos of him with someone hot called Georgia Hills, but there are none. I check his list of friends. There is no Georgia Hills. *Weird. How can he be in a thing with her? She'd be there for sure. Perhaps Maddy's wrong; she has to be... Why say that?*

I smile, buzzing inside that it's back on, and I send Holly a friend request even though it grates a little, but what the hell – she knows everyone and obviously accepts every request so before you know it Facebook will announce we are friends and my name will appear on 1,007 timelines, including Gabriel Walker's.

Downstairs, I watch Susannah and Alicia eat their kale and quinoa. *No wonder Nicholas never rushes home.* He's not back by the time Alicia goes to bed either and after I've sat in the snug (the small TV room off the kitchen) for a while, I make out I have work to do and go back upstairs to check my phone in peace.

Facebook: Holly's accepted my friend request and Maddy and Carina have sent me requests, which I now accept. Nothing from Gabriel so far, but at least there's a good chance he now knows my name.

Again, I relive it all: the good bits, the bad bits, the best bit and then comes the screaming and I can't make it stop.

The inky black sky dilutes to the grey and pink of a winter sunrise. I am back here at the riverside – no more than a bench.

You've got to let it go, Lionel says.

*That's easy for you to say. You try reliving my life every night.*

My dear, I feel like I already have. I hear you laugh, I hear you sing and that's all fine, in fact, I like your singing, what a voice, but the screaming – that's intolerable. Really, it's as if Edvard Munch has moved in next door.

I think of Munch's painting of a man holding his face as he screams. His expression agonised as he's stuck in that one miserable moment.

*You mean* The Scream*?* I ask.

That's the one.

*I get your point, but I don't know what I can do about it.*

One has obviously suffered, Lionel says. I sense your ending was particularly traumatic and I'm sorry if that's the case, but one must find a way to accept what is.

*You mean get over yourself?*

I wouldn't put it quite like that, but yes, if you like.

*But, every night it's like it's happening all over again.*

It may well help to talk about it, Lionel says.

*Nah, it's best I forget,* I say, rather than admit the truth.

# EIGHT

Blue sky brings people out. A female jogger with earphones runs by and there's another running with her dog. A man with a laptop case pauses to light a cigarette, reads the plaque and points his phone at the encryption code. There follows the usual: my name, the cringeworthy photos, and me singing my favourite Amy Winehouse song.

The man's about my dad's age (old) and he's wearing a raincoat. He drags heavily on a cigarette as he watches the website film which cuts to Mum drivelling on about her great loss, blah blah. A lump rises in my non-existent throat. It's difficult to watch and made worse by the fact it keeps repeating as if Mum's forever trapped in her grief.

The man coughs and I can hardly hear the next bit.

It's Susannah dressed in black. Nicholas is behind her in a dark suit and my sister Alicia is in a grey wool coat. It's my funeral. Despite the man's coughing I catch a sentence or two, something like, 'We're so proud of how Ren adapted to London life and her new college…'

The man has a coughing fit.

*Give it up, mate, the fags are killing you, and you don't want to end up like Lionel and me.*

Susannah continues, 'We all find ourselves longing to talk to Ren… We wish we'd had more time….' And that's the last I hear of her on film, as the man walks away.

You look lovely in that dress, Lionel says.

*Thanks.*

Delicate features – sweet little face – a touch of the Jean Seberg about you.

*Who's that?*

She was an actress in the Fifties and Sixties.

*What do you look like?*

As I understand it – an old grey bench that is slowly but visibly rotting away.

*No, I mean before. You've seen me in the video singing and stuff but I have no idea what you look like.*

Should I recall my younger self when I was at my physical peak or do I describe the ailing shell of a man that I became?

*The thing is, I've probably just lumped together all the old men I've ever known and come up with an imaginary idea of you.*

So you do see me as old.

*You have to be at least "trombones" – to me anyhow. It's not like I'm talking to another seventeen-year-old.*

Trombones. Well, perhaps I should be grateful to halt at seventy-six, rather than continue to crumble to the inevitable decrepitude of ninety-eight.

*There's nothing like being positive.*

I had thick blonde hair and bright blue eyes as a young child, but my hair darkened over time.

*Did you go bald?*

I always had a good head of hair, although it was completely white at the end.

*That's not so bad – especially with blue eyes. How tall?*

Six foot in my prime, though unfortunately I did shrink a little in old age.

*Were you fit?*

I was very sporty in my youth. I liked athletics, and played cricket and tennis.

*Yeah, but were you hot?*

Hot?

*You know – good-looking, handsome.*

Handsome, yes, it has been said.

*What a big head.*

What is that song I keep hearing? Lionel asks.

You Know I'm No Good – *it's by Amy Winehouse.*

I don't know Amy Winehouse.

*She's dead now.*

Like the best of us, my dear, like the best of us. What sort of music is it?

*She described herself as a jazz singer, but I guess she modernised it.*

I like jazz.

*She's the best. I so miss hearing her music – well, all music really.*

I'd very much like to hear more. Will you sing for me?

Instantly, my phantom heart beats faster at the thought of all I have lost.

*I don't think so*, I say.

Lionel sighs, and says, Why ever not?

*I dunno, sorry, it feels awkward for some reason.*

We have to make our own entertainment, you know.

*Yeah, I get that.*

You wanted to be a singer?

*Yeah – past tense – it's all over now.*

Go on, sing for me. You have a captive audience – it'll make my day.

*Really, that's all it takes?*

Yes, I am easy to please.

*All right, what the hell, OK, this is my all-time number one favourite song* – You Know I'm No Good. And I go for it, thinking I'll just sing the first verse, but once I start I can't stop. I don't want to, and I don't even care whether Lionel likes it or not.

Meanwhile, a skinny young bearded man wearing headphones pauses by the bench. He scratches his head, takes off his headphones, shakes them and puts them back on. He stares at the bench while I sing.

Splendid, Lionel says. I like this Amy Winehouse very much. And more to the point, I enjoyed your rendition. You sing extremely well.

The skinny bearded bloke leans in closer to read the bench's plaque. He points his phone and clicks on the link. Cue photos and the film of me singing. The bearded guy's eyes are wide. He shakes his head like he's totally freaked, and hurries away in a walk that turns into a jog.

*Was it something I said?*

Perhaps he heard you.

*He obviously didn't like it.*

He didn't like the inexplicable glimpse of otherness that it suggested.

*That's understandable.*

Indeed. Everyone wonders from time to time about what, if anything, survives after you've gone and the truth is, it wouldn't help to know.

*What music do you like, Lionel?*

It was all big bands, jazz and boogie-woogie in my day. Dizzy Gillespie, Charlie Parker and Charles Mingus were particular favourites, but I also liked Peggy Lee and Ella Fitzgerald and the songs of Cole Porter.

*Like what?*

Let me see – have you heard *Every Time We Say Goodbye*? Songwriting doesn't get much better than that.

*My Nanna always sings* Oh, What A Beautiful Morning. *So embarrassing.*

Ha, Howard Keel, I know.

*She likes show tunes.*

How old is your Nanna?

*Eighty-nine. She's devastated she's outlived me. She looked so frail at the funeral. I thought burying me might kill her and that would make Mum even worse. Nanna needs to hang on for Mum's sake.*

What about your grandad or rather grandads?

*My grandad, as in my mum's dad, died when I was five. He smoked a lot. He was funny and always singing – that's where I get it from.*

What about your other grandad?

*I never met him.*

Oh?

*I only recently met my dad.*

I'm sorry.

*Yeah, I lost out on grandads. Maybe you're here to make up for it.*

One can always find a reason if one is that way inclined.

*You mean that there's most likely no reason?*

Susannah's back with the dogs and she's brought my sister, Alicia, who's wearing her riding gear. It must be Saturday because Alicia always rides on Saturdays.

'We can't stop long,' Susannah says, as George cocks his leg by my leg.

*Beat it, George*, I say in a gruff tone that sounds like a bark.

'Shush, I'm reading.' Alicia studies the plaque. 'What's this code for?' she says, as she runs her finger over the black on metal encryption code.

'It connects to that website I showed you.'

'The one where we're at the funeral?'

'Yes, and there are all those lovely photos of Ren.'

'So anyone can hear Ren sing?'

'That's right – if they have a smartphone.'

Alicia nods, as if she's happy about that. 'Can I have your phone?'

'Not now, sweetheart, we don't have time.'

'But I want to see Ren.'

'Darling, you can watch it any time at home.'

'I miss Ren.' Alicia pouts as she sits down. 'I'm too sad to go riding now.'

'That's why I didn't want to bring you here today. I knew you'd get upset.'

'But you said it's good to express your feelings.'

'Yes, it is.'

'I want to be close to Ren.'

'You are, sweetie, and you always will be.'

'I want to see if she's here in some way.'

'Honey, it's just a bench.' Susannah sighs. 'Sitting here all day won't bring Ren back. We have to go now.'

Alicia grips the edge of the bench's seat. 'I don't want to.' She stares ahead at the river and the weeping willows.

'We're going to be late, and they're picking the gymkhana teams today.'

'I can't leave Ren here all alone.' Alicia blinks repeatedly.

'She's not going to be alone – she has visitors coming, I told you.'

*Gabe's coming?* I say. *You called Gabe? Oh, Susannah, thank you, I knew you'd do that for me.*

The dogs bark.

'George, Max – that will do,' Susannah says. 'Alicia, we have to go. I'll bring you back tomorrow when we'll have more time.'

'You promise?'

'Yes, we'll bring flowers. You can make it pretty.'

'Can we get black flowers?'

'I was thinking of some nice white lilies.'

'Ren likes black.'

Susannah takes hold of Alicia's hands and pulls her up from the bench. 'Come on, sweetheart, we need to go.'

They walk away and Alicia looks back and waves.

*Did you hear that, Lionel? I've got a visitor coming. It'll be Gabriel, I know it.*

That's marvellous news. Tell me, was that your little sister?

*Yeah. Alicia.*

How old is she?

*She's ten, or she could be eleven. Her birthday's just after Christmas and something tells me I've definitely missed Christmas.*

She's very fond of you.

*Yeah, I guess.*

Have you always got on well?

*Yeah, but we've only known each other a little while.*

Ah, silly me, I should have thought.

*She's my half-sister.*

How was it when you first met?

*She wasn't there the first night. Susannah arranged for her to sleep over at a friend's house straight from school. I think she wanted her safely out of the way in case I wasn't who I said I was.*

Understandable in the circumstances – a mother must protect her child.

*Yeah, well, I thought she was being a bitch.*

But you met the following day?

*Yeah. I got up late and no one was around so I pigged out in the kitchen – I can't help myself sometimes and then I felt fat. It's a girl thing, trust me – and I just looked at the swimming pool and thought I've got to go in and work it all off. And even though I didn't have a costume with me, I thought, what the hell, I'm the only one here. Who's to know?*

Where were they all?

*Susannah had gone to collect Alicia and my dad does these stupid long bike rides, like sixty kilometres or more so he's always out. Anyway, I got undressed and found a towel to wrap around me, although to be honest it barely covered my arse, checked no one was around, and dived in. The pool is sick. I was always planning how I'd have a party there and get all my mates up from Devon…*

I'm so sorry, Lionel says.

*Yeah, well, whatever, it wasn't to be.*

I watch the river, imagining I can dissolve into it and be washed away. It's no good, I can't think like that. I shake the thought away.

*Anyway, like I said, everyone was out so I swam for a bit then messed about playing dead, and when I came back up I heard the dogs barking and wondered what had set them off.*

*'Are you a chav?' someone said, and I immediately ducked my shoulders down beneath the water before looking around to find this girl, as in Alicia, staring at me.*

I'm confused, Lionel says. What does "chav" mean?

*It's like young and common, you know, a bit yobbish with no taste.*

That's not so good.

*Yeah, I know right, and it gets worse. I pleaded with Alicia to pass me the towel I'd left on one of the loungers, but she just goes, 'You're naked. Why are you naked? And you've got a tattoo? Daddy says only chavs have tattoos.'*

Some mistake surely, Lionel says.

*No, I have got a tattoo. Loads of people have them.*

Do they really? How extraordinary. It was only sailors and convicts in my day and certainly not women, not respectable women anyway.

*I'd say about a quarter of young people have them now.*

Good heavens, as many as that?

*You can get some amazing ones. Anyway, I asked her not to tell anyone because I'd had it done illegally – you're supposed to be eighteen.*

*I said, 'My mate did it and I wouldn't want to get him in trouble because he's one of my bezzies, know what I mean?' And I winked, and she shrugged.*

*'Alicia, please get me the towel?'*

*Finally, she picked up my towel and said, 'That won't cover you up. It's tiny.' And she walked off then, and I was panicking, but thankfully she returned with this really thick, fluffy towel and I got out as quick as I could and wrapped it around me making sure I completely covered up my tattoo.*

Did Susannah mind you having a swim?

*She did say don't swim naked again, and that if I'd just asked she'd have found me a costume, and she then went off and came back with fresh clothes because I hadn't brought any.*

Why ever not?

*When I left Devon, it wasn't planned. It was more a reaction to something that happened. I told you that.*

I'm sorry, my dear, my memory isn't what it was. Tell me again.

*It's all very boring, but if you must know, I went to college one day (this was back at home in Devon), and my best mate Kemi showed me her phone and there was this video clip going around. Everyone had seen it apart from me and it was of my then boyfriend Griff with another girl and it was totally gross – boobs showing and everything. And I just flipped out and left.*

Slow down. Video clip on a phone – you've lost me?

*You know a smartphone?*

You mean those wallet-sized devices that people stare at constantly?

*Yeah, smartphones – everyone has them.*

People don't even look where they're going. I can only assume these devices contain the very meaning of life.

*Well, you can get messages and play games and take photos.*

They weren't around when I passed.

*You never had a mobile phone?*

The technology must have been in its infancy and far too expensive.

*People used to have massive phones, didn't they – the size of bricks?*

I remember walkie-talkies.

*Did you even have a TV?*

Very funny. Yes, I did, although not until 1960, and it was black and white.

*You are truly ancient.*

I'll ignore that. So, you left college?

*I left everything – just walked out of my whole life.*

You ran away?

*I guess you could say that. I walked out of college, emptied my bank account and caught the first train to London.*

And you went to your father's house?

*Yeah, as in the dad I'd never met.*

Why hadn't you met?

*I don't know. My mum never talked about him. And whenever I asked she'd just get moody.*

But you knew where he lived?

*Yeah, I'd found out a few weeks beforehand. There was this letter in my mum's drawer. She must have wanted me to see it, or she wouldn't have left it there, because she knew I borrowed her things and it wasn't there before.*

What did it say?

*It was from his solicitor checking on whether I was still in education and it included his address. I memorised it and Googled it.*

Googled it? You've lost me, I don't understand.

*Wow, you have been dead a long time. Google's a search engine.*

A search engine – are we talking trains now?

*No, never mind, it doesn't matter. Back to when I met Alicia. Like I said, I hadn't brought any clothes or anything so Susannah made me change into these butters jogging bottoms and a sweatshirt.*

Butters?

*It means ugly.*

Well, beggars can't be choosers.

*Yeah, all right, and then I wanted to see my dad, but he wasn't back yet so Susannah made Alicia show me the garden.*

And what's that like?

*It's wicked. There's even a lake, which my dad calls Lake Bonus – tacky, I know, but he's a banker. And there's a massive lawn and a maze. Alicia pretends the maze is made up of roads and that she's driving away, but I always think why would you drive away when you live there?*

Quite.

*I felt jealous, like I'd lost out somehow. I told Alicia how lucky she was and she said, 'Well, you can live here now you've found us. We've plenty of room,' which I thought was really sweet of her.*

You must have been the luckiest runaway in England.

*Yeah, really, and to think I could've been on the streets if Susannah hadn't answered the buzzer.*

What about your father? You haven't told me anything about meeting him.

*I can't go into that right now.*

But you've barely mentioned him.

*I know,* I say, my voice cracking. *It's just I have visitors.*

# NINE

There's incredible warmth. All is grey and dull and yet it's as if the sun's beating down warming every inch of my phantom skin.

It's Mum and my baby brother Jay, though he's not so much the 'baby' these days. He looks taller and stronger than I remember, while Mum seems smaller. She's dressed in a black wool coat with a thick black scarf and Jay's wearing a hoodie and puffa jacket.

*Mum, Jay, it's so good to see you.* I go to them, hug and kiss them, but they don't hug me back. Why not? I hate that, I think, as I shrink away.

They stop in front of the bench and stare.

Mum's hair's greying at the roots. She's let that go. *You need to sort that, Mum.* She looks weepy. I wish she wouldn't. I'm bored of all that. I want jokes, fun times – *Jay, make me laugh.* He pulls up his hood and half hides his face.

*What's that all about? It's not as if anyone knows you.*

Oh, hold on, I get it – Mum has a small stuffed white bear with a love heart on its belly.

*Do not put that thing anywhere near me,* I say, but she does anyway – wedging it right into the corner of the seat so it won't fall off.

Jeez, a cuddly bear – I look even more tragic.

Mum stands back. Why do all the adults in my life do that? It's like they have to appreciate the bench as if it's a work of art.

'It is a lovely bench,' she says, and Jay shrugs.

*Yeah, that's right, bro. A bench is a bench.*

'It must be teak,' Mum says. 'Nicholas always buys quality.'

'It's the least he can do,' Jay says.

'Look at the plaque – is that stainless steel?'

'Well, I doubt it's platinum.'

'It's nicely done,' Mum says, 'lovely engraving.'

Jay curls his lip. 'That's not right. They should have put Ren in brackets at least. She hated the name Lauren.'

*See, Jay knows – love you, bro.*

'I know,' Mum says. 'If I'd ordered it I'd have included "Ren". Perhaps we should get another bench down in Bovey – somewhere for us to go regularly – maybe in the graveyard or near the park? I'll make sure that says "Ren".'

*No way, not another bench. What are you going to do, split me in two – half up here in London and half in Devon?*

'I've got to test it.' Jay gets out his phone and clicks on the code. 'There's my sis.' He laughs. 'What a fat baby.'

'Bonny is the word,' Mum says.

'And there's one with me on holiday.'

'That was Cornwall.'

'That's Ren and Kemi on Haytor. And that's us the Christmas before last.'

It cuts to me singing in that black lacy dress at Holly Appleby's party.

'She looks pretty there,' Jay says.

Mum nods. 'She does, doesn't she, but it's so hard to hear her sing – that voice, so pure, angelic even.' Mum sounds croaky. 'Turn it off now.'

And they sit down, like everyone has before them. It's as if you can't visit a memorial bench without sitting on it.

*Anyhow, where's Billy?* I ask about Mum's loser boyfriend. *Could he not get a day off from being unemployed?*

Mum pushes a wisp of hair off her face. 'It's a nice spot. Look at that view. I like that big old tree and the weeping willows. Oh, look at that little dog.' She points at a small fluffy thing that thankfully doesn't pay me a visit.

Jay frowns. 'It's not the sort of place you'd associate with Ren though. I know this is London, but it's quiet, more like the countryside and she'd had enough of that.'

'I wish she'd never come to London,' Mum says. 'None of this would have happened. I wish she'd never met that…'

*That what? What does she mean?*

Mum stifles a sob and Jay puts his arm around her as she doubles over, a folded-up lump in a black wool coat.

'It is what it is,' Jay says. 'At least that piece of shit has been charged.'

*Oh my God.* I can hardly believe what I'm hearing. The police must have sorted it. I knew they would but, wow, that's fast work.

Mum sits back up. 'There's no need to swear, you know I don't like that.'

'It's not like you disagree, Mum.'

Her jaw tenses. 'I can't believe we have to wait so long for this court case. Why do these things take so long? It's ridiculous, it really is. I need some sort of closure, not that it will bring Ren back but it will help.'

'We have to hang in there. We will get justice for Ren, I'll make sure of that.'

*Jay, you're amazing. I always knew you had my back.*

'I still can't get my head around it,' Mum says. 'I know we didn't meet him, but from what everyone said I thought he was good for her – calmed her down. Nicholas said he studies hard and is very bright.'

Jay shakes his head. 'Doesn't mean he's not a psycho.'

*What?* I don't get what they're saying.

Jay curls his lip. 'I don't care what anyone says, he's scum.'

*I don't get it.*

'She thought she was in love and that makes me especially sad and angry. I hate to think of her being taken in by that boy.'

*What are you saying, Mum?*

Jay clenches his fists. 'Gabriel Walker's going down for sure and if for some stupid reason he doesn't, I'll get him anyway.'

*What? You're talking rubbish. It wasn't Gabe – he'd never do anything like that. He loves me. I love him. You've got it all wrong. This is madness.*

'It just goes to show you can never tell,' Mum says.

*He didn't do it*, I shout, or at least I think I do. It's like I'm stuck in a bad dream where my love is in danger and I need to shout out to save him but instantly, inexplicably, I'm rendered mute.

'It's gone cold all of a sudden,' Mum says. 'Do you feel it or is it just me?'

'Yeah, freezing. It's no fun sitting here.'

'I don't think I can stay much longer even though we haven't been here long.'

'Don't worry, Mum. We'll be back soon enough.'

*Wait, Mum, listen – it wasn't Gabriel.*

Mum looks down at me, her eyes glassy. 'We've got to go, my darling, but we'll see you next week after the memorial service. Love you so much – always will.' She leans over and kisses the stupid plaque that bears my full name like a passport that can't take me anywhere.

# TEN

I have never felt so stuck fast, trapped within the freshly stained wood as I watch Mum and Jay walk away.

*Mum, it wasn't Gabriel,* I shout. *He'd never do that. He loves me. You've got to believe me. We've got to help him. If he goes down, it'll be a miscarriage of justice.*

They glance back, their faces serious, and Jay puts his arm around Mum.

*Mum, Jay, listen, it wasn't Gabe. Believe me. He loves me.*

*Mum, Jay – wait.*

The sky turns metallic grey with the threat of rain.

*No,* I shout and cry, *you've got to listen to me. It wasn't Gabe.*

And the more I shout, the faster they walk.

*It wasn't Gabe.*

I think back and see his face and who else?

Who was it?

Why can't I remember? I have a vague impression of what happened – the specific reason slightly beyond reach – but I do know it wasn't Gabe. *It wasn't Gabe.*

For goodness sake, Ren, stop shouting, Lionel says. You must learn to channel it or you'll never break through.

*Lionel, leave it. I'm not in the mood.*

I'm only trying to help.

*You can't help – no one can. Look, I don't mean to be rude but I've just found out that my boyfriend has been charged for something he didn't do. How the hell can you help with that?*

Is this to do with your death?

*Yes.*

Was he involved in any way?

*No.*

You would know.

*Yeah, exactly, I would know – I was there.*

My dear, you need to improve your communication skills. You must learn to break through. Although, I must say, you do seem to have a certain aptitude for it already.

*I don't get what you mean.*

My dear, a new bench always receives extra visitors. They come from far and wide, relieved to have a focus for contemplation and somewhere pleasant to ease their grief. With you, however, they do not sit long. This is most unusual, especially when loved ones have travelled far. My guess is that they sense your torment – perhaps some of this screaming is indeed breaking through.

*What d'you mean?*

It's almost as if you're the screaming bench.

*What the hell?*

I likened you to the Munch painting at first, but now I'm thinking Francis Bacon's *Screaming Pope* series. Have you seen them? They depict absolute anguish.

I think of the contorted faces in the Bacon paintings.

But if one can calm it down, stop screaming as it were, who knows what can be achieved?

*What are you saying?*

You can talk to the living.

*Are you for real?*

You need a receptive listener, and it will take a serious level of concentration on your part, but I think you can do it.

*Are you saying I can haunt people?*

Call it that if you like.

*Can you haunt people?*

I have broken through on occasion, yes.

*What happened?*

Lionel sighs. It wasn't as successful as I hoped.

*Why, who was it? What happened?*

There were issues with my daughter and I'm happy to talk about it, but for now let's concentrate on you.

The river is steely grey. People walk by: a man and a small child, and a woman with a pram. Cyclists, dog walkers and the occasional drunk – the opportunities to talk are limited as there are so many benches lining the riverside, each and every one tragic in its own way, and only the odd random person picks me. I have an urgent message and I need to reach the next friend, relative or stranger who sits here. I need to let them, someone, anyone know that it wasn't Gabriel.

*You're right – I must break through, what do I need to do?*

It's not something one can teach.

*Are you winding me up?*

I would say it's all about practice.

*I haven't got time for that.* A flush of panic rises within me.

It's a craft, an art even, something you have to master and that takes time and effort. At the moment, you merely express your alarm and that pushes people away. You need to ensure that the correct message breaks through.

I think back to all the singing practice I did: the hours spent alone in my room singing scales and doing voice exercises. I practised, I gigged and where did it get me? *Am I in hell? Because it sure feels like it right now.*

My dear, we all carry our own troubles as we do our triumphs.

The sun sets and the riverside darkens apart from the lamps a little further down. Lionel quietens as he always does around dusk. I dread the darkness, and yet at the same time look forward to meeting Gabriel again as if it were the first time.

# ELEVEN

I see Gabe. His soft hazel eyes meet mine and the heart I feared had been turned to stone flutters once again. 'He's in a thing with someone.' Maddy crushes my dreams, only it turns out she hasn't because I later realise she's wrong. Gabe's as free as me and hope re-enters my new London life.

It's my second day at Bourne's and my form tutor Mrs Anders, an old-school battle-axe in a pussy-bow blouse, is on my case. 'Laura, we discussed the dress code yesterday and yet once again your outfit does not pass as office wear.'

*I'm seventeen. I dress seventeen. That means leggings, band T-shirt, baggy cardigan and leather jacket, but more to the point my name is not Laura.* 'My name's Ren,' I say, but the old trout merely peers over her glasses and tells me my hairstyle and clothes are "inappropriate".

'It's my basic human right to dress and look how I want.'

She gives me the evils, but lets it go for the day.

Maddy, Carina, lunchtime, Chicken Shack and this time I go for the smaller box of chicken. We sit at the same table as yesterday on the left-hand side, and soon have only a few chicken bones and beakers of watery Coke between us, when in walk Aaron and *the others*.

Again, Gabriel is last. He looks straight at me and my heart jolts like it must have stopped post-Griff and has now been kick-started. We both say 'All right', though I'm not sure the word actually comes out of my mouth in any audible sense.

At the counter, they mess around and keep looking back.

'Are you sure Gabriel's seeing someone?' I ask Maddy.

She looks askance, and says, 'That's what I heard.'

'Someone told you that?' I want to get to the bottom of whether she's been misinformed.

'Can't remember.' She looks away, closing the conversation, and I let it go.

The lads sit at the next table. Aaron says 'Hello' on behalf of all of them, and Carina sits up all pert while Maddy eyes them with a faint smile.

Gabriel's furthest away and at a diagonal in my direct line of vision. I like that I can see him so clearly, but at the same time it's awkward, so as a distraction I suck on my straw and take a mouthful of watery Coke.

'Who's the new girl?' Aaron asks Maddy, while nodding towards me.

'This is Ren. She's from Devon.'

I brace myself ready for jokes about shagging sheep, but instead Aaron introduces everyone starting with the skinny lad opposite. 'This is James,' he says, and then looks to his right at the freckle-faced redhead. 'That's Fenton, and the ugly one there, that's Gabriel.' Aaron winks at Maddy and she smiles while narrowing her eyes as if there's a private joke.

'I've been to Devon. We did a survival course,' Aaron says. 'They dumped us in the middle of nowhere with a map and compass and we had to find our way back.'

'Did you make it?' I ask.

'Nah, we had to call for help and it was freezin' and it rained all the time.'

'It rains a lot.'

'D'you surf?' The one with freckles asks.

'Yeah, I have – in Cornwall.'

'Not Devon?'

'I live in the middle near Dartmoor.'

'It's the only county with two non-consecutive coastlines,' Gabriel says.

'Here he goes, Nerd-boy strikes again,' Aaron says.

'Shut up.'

Aaron changes the subject. 'I hear there's a party comin' up – Holly Appleby's – you all goin'?'

'It's her eighteenth,' Carina says.

'She hangs with the bitchy group,' Maddy says, 'not sure she'll invite us.'

'When is it?' Gabriel asks, and I take the chance to look at him for a moment.

'I think it's soon,' Carina says. 'I heard her talking about it the other day.'

'She's been going on about it for months,' Maddy says.

'You'll let us know?' Aaron says. 'I reckon it'll be kickin'.'

'What makes you think she'll invite you?' Maddy says.

'I'll turn up whatever.'

'Don't think that'll work. She'll have security on the door.'

'She'll want us there,' Aaron says. 'Fit single lads are always welcome.'

I look across at Gabriel. And he looks back, his soft hazel eyes holding mine for as long as I can bear it before looking away and then back again.

'Dartmoor's famous for its tors,' he says, glancing at Maddy and then me.

'What are tors?' James asks.

'They're like rocky hilltops,' he says.

'They're made of granite,' I say, 'there's loads of them.'

'Aren't there like Bronze Age settlements?' Gabriel says.

'Yeah, you can still see the hut circles made from rocks.'

Fenton throws a chicken bone at Gabriel. 'Why you talkin' about rocks?'

'We did walk past that kind of thing on that trip.'

'It's all borin',' Aaron says.

Maddy checks the time on her phone. 'We better go.'

'Hey, country girl.' Aaron's looking at me. 'Facebook me, yeah?'

'Facebook you?'

He winks. 'You like me, yeah.'

'I think she's had it with boys right now,' Maddy says.

'You gay?' Aaron asks.

I burn up and say, 'I've just finished with someone.'

'What, like a girl?'

'It wouldn't matter if it was,' Carina says.

Maddy curls her lip. 'You're such a Neanderthal, Aaron.'

'Yeah, grow up,' Carina says, as she glances back at Idris.

I want to get out into the fresh air, while inside I'm gutted that Gabriel may now think I'm not interested in anyone. Maddy makes a move and we follow.

Outside, I glance back through the window looking for Gabriel. I see him and he sees me. I look away and then back again and he's staring in a good way, his soft hazel eyes lock with mine, and it's like the rest of the world blurs. *Facebook me.*

I create a chart on the back of my English folder entitled GSC – short for Gabriel Sightings Chart. There are three columns: one has a drawing of a chicken for Chicken Shack, one has a bus and the third is for random sightings that could occur anywhere. *I like him, he likes me – what could be easier?*

I live for Chicken Shack and a pattern to my new London life emerges:

Bus to college – fair chance of seeing Gabriel.

College – daily grief from Anders-the-trout re what I'm wearing, whatever I'm wearing, but I am what I am so she can swivel. No chance of seeing Gabriel.

Lunch – Chicken Shack – most likely to see Gabriel.

Bus home – good chance of seeing Gabriel.

* * *

Thursday, Chicken Shack, and Idris gives Carina the biggest smile. I swear that girl literally runs to the counter and invites him out for coffee. They swap numbers.

'We'll never hear the last of this,' Maddy says.

'You might need to buy that hat after all.'

We're sitting on the left-hand side as usual and we eat our chicken but there's no sign of Gabriel or his mates.

On the way out, Carina waves to Idris making the sign of a phone at her ear as if to say "Call me". Outside, Aaron, James and Fenton are on their way, but there's no Gabriel. He's not on the bus home either. *Is he ill?* I can't ask.

Back at Ambrose House there's the heavy, awkward sound of a cello being abused. Alicia's in the Blue Room having her weekly lesson. I poke my head around the door and make a face.

In the distance, through the patio doors there are men pulling at the plants. Susannah's got the gardeners in. There are loads of them, a whole team. It's warm for late September and one of the younger ones has his shirt off. He catches my eye and smiles, while I think, don't – you are not Gabriel.

# TWELVE

Chicken Shack, a day later, and in walks Gabriel with Fenton.

Gabriel has a black eye. *How did that happen?* There's little chance they'll sit near us, not without loudmouth Aaron to help them along, but I look anyhow and Gabriel does meet my eye at one point. Absently, he touches his bruised face and looks away. He and Fenton buy take-outs and leave.

*I like him, he likes me – how hard can it be?* From a promising start, it feels as if Gabriel has moved out of reach. And worse, the invites to Holly Appleby's eighteenth are out and, being her 1,008th Facebook friend, I haven't made the guest-list.

Lunchtime, Friday – Chicken Shack, table on the right-hand side for a change and Aaron, James, Fenton and Gabriel sit at the adjoining table. *Things are looking up.*

Gabriel looks straight at me. 'We *have* been invited to Holly's party – you're all goin', yeah?' He glances at Maddy and Carina and then back at me. 'So you've not?'

'Told you *we'd* be on the guest list,' Aaron says.

'I heard she's booked the worst DJ,' Maddy says. 'It's gonna be a dead session.'

'You're chattin' shit,' Aaron says.

I shrug and say, 'She knows too many people.'

Maddy nods. 'Definitely too many girls, and all bitches.'

'Sour grapes, innit,' Aaron says.

'Maybe she hasn't asked everyone yet,' Gabriel says.

Maddy says, 'I'll wangle an invite one way or another.'

* * *

That evening I call up Facebook on my phone, click through to Gabriel's page and, *what the hell*, I send a friend request.

Saturday. Susannah insists on a family day out, but at least it's Westfield – shopping in other words. Nicholas comes down to breakfast dressed in Lycra and Susannah pulls a face. 'Why are you wearing that?'

I laugh and say, 'I know, butters, right.'

'I'm doing 60k today – Surrey Hills, I told you.'

'What a freak,' I say under my breath.

'You're not cycling,' Susannah says. 'We're going to Westfield.'

'I *love* Westfield,' Alicia says.

'What are you on about?' Nicholas says.

'I told you last night, we're having a family day out. It's the least you can do after coming home so late.'

'As I explained, I was out with clients – hardly enjoyable. I've had a hard week. I need the cycling to de-stress.'

'Ren needs a new wardrobe. It's the easiest way to stop that teacher going on at her.'

'She was shopping online the other day.'

'Did you see what she bought? She spent her entire allowance on a hideous second-hand leather jacket. She needs guidance.'

'It's vintage. I thought you liked it,' I say, a bit put out because the jacket's banging – sort of Sixties style with a little collar and cute leather-covered buttons.

'Her whole allowance?' Nicholas says.

'I've always wanted a leather jacket.'

Nicholas ignores that and says, 'Shopping's your thing. You all go.' But Susannah moves up close and whispers in his ear, and the only words I catch are "bonding" and "session". He's so beaten and he knows it, as he sighs heavily and retreats upstairs to change.

I check Facebook on my phone. *Gabriel – accept my request.*

Nicholas reappears in jeans, shirt and a V-neck Ralph Lauren jumper and we take Susannah's shiny white Range Rover to shiny Westfield, which is massive with loads of shops I've never been to.

'I'm going to sort school shoes for Alicia,' Susannah says. 'I suggest we split for a while and you two head off together.'

Time for a "bonding session" in other words, but within minutes of entering Top Shop Nicholas pisses me off. 'The noise in this place,' he says, as he grimaces at a dress I'm holding. 'You're not wearing that.'

'Why are you being so negative?'

He shakes his head. 'I'll be back.' He walks out and I'm glad to get rid of him until I remember he's got the cash.

Whatever. I try on loads of items in the hope someone will come back and pay for some of them. And I check my phone every other minute. It keeps pinging with messages, only none of them are the message I want.

Nicholas returns and passes me some cash. 'I'll be outside.' He can't be arsed, so I'm left to choose what the hell I like. *Result.* I buy a sweatshirt, black jeans, short skirt, and the cutest party dress ever, even though I have no party to go to any time soon.

Nicholas calls. 'Yo! Sushi now – we have seats. Don't tell Susannah I let you choose everything.'

My phone pings. It's a text from Maddy: 'Hurry – Aaron etc are here'.

I text back: 'Have to go eat sushi'. I'm gutted. *Gabriel's here in Westfield too and I have to hang out with my family.*

At Yo! Sushi, Nicholas, Susannah and Alicia are seated at the conveyor belt.

'D'you like my new shoes?' Alicia holds up a shoebox containing plimsolls that look like they've been dipped in glue, glitter and sequins.

'They're a crime against high-tops.'

'She's not wearing those to school,' Nicholas says.

'They're for home, stupid,' Alicia says.

'Don't call your father "stupid",' Susannah says, and turns to me. 'What have you bought?'

It won't go well, but still I take out my new sweatshirt, jeans, Nirvana T-shirt and black dress. 'Banging, aren't they?'

'It all looks the same as the clothes you already have. You need to look smart for college. Nicholas, I did tell you.'

Susannah takes me around loads more shops until I give in and agree to a black pleated skirt, two shirts and a cardigan.

'You're trying to stop me from being me. I like what I wear. That's what I feel comfortable in – just let me be happy.'

'You're making life harder for yourself,' she says. 'You need to meet them halfway, compromise and I promise they'll leave you alone.'

*Compromise?* She knows nothing about teenagers.

At last, once I agree to Susannah's selection of clothes, they all head home and I finally get to meet my friends.

'Hey, Ren.' Carina waves as soon as she spots me.

'About time,' Maddy says, and we all hug like we've known each other ages.

'Where are Aaron and the others?' I ask, and they burst out laughing.

'Lol,' Carina says. 'We knew you'd hurry up if we said Aaron and *the others* were here – Maddy's idea.'

'They've got football,' Maddy says, 'sorry to disappoint you, but it's just us.'

We spend an hour walking around the shops looking at stuff we can't afford while trying to catch the eye of boys we are unlikely ever to know.

'This is boring,' I say. 'Where else can we go?'

We're at Westfield's main entrance and it's raining.

I check my phone – still no Gabriel.

'I've got to head off anyhow,' Carina says.

Maddy curls her lip. 'She's ditching us.'

'Idris?' I say.

Maddy nods. 'Traitor,' she says in a low voice, like she means it.

'It's not like that,' Carina says, 'that's why I met you guys first. You know I always put you first.'

My phone pings – a text message. Susannah wants me back within an hour. *What is her problem?*

'D'you want to come back to mine?' I ask Maddy, as it's easier than explaining that like a complete loser I've got to get back early.

We catch the tube and a bus and then run in the rain up the lane towards Ambrose House. 'Is this a short cut?' Maddy asks, as she stares up at the houses that are all named rather than numbered. 'You don't live in one of these?' She frowns.

We're at the gates of Ambrose House. I key in the code.

The dogs are barking.

'What have you got in there?'

'Hound of the Baskervilles, only worse, there's two of them.' I open the door and the dogs run at Maddy. 'George, Max, beat it.'

'Get off, I hate dogs.' Maddy backs away by the hall table.

'George, Max, down.' They chill a little, circling the room with their tails wagging. 'Sorry, they get super-excited.'

Maddy brushes herself down, her jaw tense, as she looks around at the high ceiling, ornate mirror and chequered floor. 'Quite a place.'

I take her down to the basement kitchen, where Susannah looks as surprised as Susannah can due to the Botox. 'Ren, we've been trying to get hold of you.'

'I'm not late.'

Nicholas looks up from his mobile. 'You never answer your phone. Why is that?'

'What's the problem?'

'We wanted an update – because we care,' Susannah says.

'You worry too much,' I say, 'this is Maddy, by the way.'

Susannah immediately offers Maddy one of her health-freak

juices. 'It includes acai berries,' she says.

I roll my eyes. 'Acai berries are going to save the planet.'

Maddy sips at it. 'It's nice.'

I laugh. 'You don't like it.'

'What are you studying, Maddy?'

I groan. 'You're so embarrassing.'

'Maddy, do you ever get in trouble for what you wear to college?' Susannah asks.

'Of course she doesn't,' I say. 'Look at her – she could go and work in an office today if she wanted.'

They obviously like Maddy as Susannah invites her to dinner and then to sleep over. I show her around, and she's amazed at the scale and glamour of it all. 'I'd show you the garden if it wasn't pissing down with rain,' I say, as we look out of the French windows.

'A lake?' Maddy has a deep line furrowing her brow. 'That's ridiculous.'

I laugh. 'I know, right, that's what I thought when I first saw it.'

Alicia arrives home from horse riding and Nicholas orders pizza on the quiet, explaining that the word "pizza" does not feature in Susannah's vocabulary. And we steal alcohol – who wouldn't when it's all lit up, advertising itself, in its own double fridge? 'This is too funny,' I say, as we wait for Nicholas and Susannah to go to bed. 'Nicholas will go up first as he's got a 60k bike ride tomorrow – the freak – and then Susannah will take the dogs out.' Nicholas goes up and the dogs are let out, and we run down and grab two bottles from the fridge.

'Are they screw-top?' Maddy asks.

I put one back and search for another. 'Got one.'

We run upstairs to the Hummingbird Suite and collapse onto the bed laughing.

'What about glasses?' Maddy says.

I go back downstairs and get glasses of water and whatever snacks I can find: popcorn and some weird red cake that may contain beetroot.

Back upstairs, Maddy says, 'Let's Skype someone. Who have you got on there?'

I shrug. 'Just Devon friends.'

'Show me.'

I call up Kemi.

'Badgers,' she says.

'Badgers,' I repeat with a smile.

'Badgers?' Maddy says.

'It's a Devon thing, I'll explain later.'

'What's up?' Kemi says.

'Just hanging at my endz with the Madster.' I raise my tumbler of wine.

'It's Maddy,' Maddy says.

'Love your onesie,' Kemi says.

Maddy's is Pokemon and mine's a tiger with a tail.

'What's been happening?' I say.

'I was round Ben's earlier.'

'You still in love?'

'Shut up.' She smiles. 'What about you? How's the singing?' I shrug, and she says, 'Have you heard her, Maddy?'

Maddy looks put out. 'I didn't know you sing.'

'Sing something now,' Kemi says.

'I'm not in the mood.'

'Do *At Last* – I love that one,' Kemi says. '*Please*.'

'Go on,' Maddy says. 'I want to hear you.'

'Yeah, come on. If you're serious about a singing career you need to practise.'

'That's right,' Maddy says. 'Practice makes perfect.'

'I can't,' I say, but then I think, *what the hell*, I've got to get used to it, so I close my eyes because everyone feels too close and I need to shut them out, get in the zone and channel Etta James and Beyoncé as I sing *At Last.* And my eyes remain shut throughout the entire song and when I open them again, I find Maddy with a faint smile on her face as she holds up her iPhone.

'Did you film me?'

Maddy grips her phone like she thinks I'll grab it. 'You're quite good.'

Kemi claps and whoops. 'What have you done about your singing since you've been in London?'

'I've been really busy with college and stuff.'

'You've done nothing? No way, I'm pissed off now.'

'Kemi, I can't even open my eyes when I sing, let alone perform in public.'

'You need to get out there. You've got to let people hear you. You can't waste the talent you have.'

'I'm going to upload this to Facebook and YouTube,' Maddy says. 'That's how Lily Allen started and I have to admit you're miles better than her.'

'I will kill you.'

'I could be your manager,' Maddy says. 'We'll go 50/50.'

'Yeah, right.'

'You need to gig.'

'I'm not ready for that.'

'I've been trying to get her to gig for years,' Kemi says. 'It'll be sick if you can get her out there. Anyhow, I'm gonna go now, leave you to your drinks and popcorn.' Kemi cuts me off before I can ask about Griff and Izzy. *What the hell.*

Maddy pours me another glass of Sancerre and we watch *Donnie Darko* on my laptop while eating beetroot cake and popcorn.

'Last glass.' Maddy empties the second bottle of wine.

'You finish it,' I say, and go to the bathroom.

'You're going to miss the end of the film,' Maddy says, but I am beyond caring as I stand doubled up over the toilet bowl, as everything I have consumed comes back up in a reddish-purple watery pulp that tastes nothing like Sancerre.

At last, Gabriel accepts my friend request and so the fact I feel beyond rubbish doesn't matter. I click through to his profile. Finally, I can find out more about him. He doesn't post much, but he's been tagged a fair amount. There are photos: Gabriel playing football, trying on hats in a shop and skateboarding. He's often in groups (girls included). He has eighty-seven friends – not many, thirty-two photos – not many at all and "likes"? He hasn't added any. *He's not into Facebook*. But at least he's on it and I can message him. I do so immediately – one word: 'Hey'.

I hear voices. People are approaching.

'This is it. I swear it's this one.'

Two young men are at the bench. One has a beard. He looks familiar. Is that the skinny guy with headphones from earlier?

His friend, who's also thin and tall, and has stubble, leans in to read the plaque, but it's too dark so he uses the light on his phone.

He clicks on the code, calling up the usual tedious photos of me, followed by Mum's eulogy and Susannah, etc.

'Heavy shit,' the guy with stubble says.

I have to agree. It's all too sad and I brace myself for a whirlpool of fresh grief at what I've lost that will drag me downwards and around, spinning to eternity.

The film cuts to the clip of me singing Amy.

The two men nod their approval.

'She's good,' stubble man says.

'She really is,' the bearded guy says.

'I'm not getting no ghost though,' Stubble says.

'Try turning it off, see if you can still hear it,' Beardy says.

They stand completely still, their heads slightly cocked to one side as if that will help them hear.

*Hello again*, I say. *You were here earlier. I really need your help.*

'Can't hear nothing, mate,' Stubble says. 'Think you need to get your head checked.' He makes a gesture as if his friend with the beard is loopy.

The bearded guy hugs himself tight. 'It's freezing.'

Stubble puts an arm around his friend's shoulders. It could be affection or it could be to steady himself. 'I reckon you clicked on that code and didn't realise.'

'Yeah, I guess I must have done.' Beardy frowns. 'Back to the pub, yeah?'

*Wait,* I shout, *you're right. I'm here. You heard me. It wasn't a recording. You heard me sing.*

They walk away talking and laughing as they shove each other across the path.

*Please – wait… Listen!* I sing a few lines and not very well. It's no good.

*Lionel, did you hear that? Remember that guy with the beard and headphones who was here earlier? He heard me. He came back. He came back because he wanted to hear me sing again. Only it didn't work. I was too late.*

Lionel remains faithful to his usual silent night, while I watch the two young men in the distance as they grow steadily smaller and disappear.

The lights on the bridge reflect in the water and a bus or two passes by, but I don't count those any more.

# THIRTEEN

I watch the dark river and wait for the dawn, desperate to talk to Lionel but I know I must let him say the first word. He's funny like that. Already I know his ways and they won't change, not now, he'd be ninety-eight if still alive, but even at seventy-six (his death age) he must have been stuck in his ways.

Am I stuck – forever seventeen? Will I always be a teenager experiencing the extreme highs and lows of all this love and pain? I never wanted to grow old. I never thought about it to be honest. Old was invisible to me, apart from Nanna.

Poor Nanna, she looked so frail at my funeral – a bundle of sticks wrapped in an oversized coat that must have fitted her at one time. I hate not being able to phone home, although to be honest I rarely did.

There are birds in the beech tree – four fat pigeons cooing to one another. The darkness lifts a little and a fuzz of frost highlights the tips of the reeds and the path's edge. It's a cold, crisp morning – people's breath will be visible on the air. I try to blow outwards, but of course I can't do that any more.

The first dog walker of the day is a man in a grey deerstalker hat with a muzzled German Shepherd. *Keep walking – piss elsewhere.* But the dog slows and sniffs at Lionel. The man tugs on the lead and the stupid mutt is then at me, cocking his furry leg. *All I need.*

I sense Lionel smiling, though of course there's nothing to see.

Another one got you, he says, with a chuckle. I must say, you're damned attractive to canines.

*Morning, Lionel,* I say, because nothing can bother me today, not now I know.

*I can do it,* I say. *I broke through.*

My dear, please give me a moment – one is not yet compos mentis.

*It's not as if you sleep.*

No, but I do go elsewhere.

*How do you mean?*

You relive your highlights and lowlights. And I, for what it's worth, relive mine.

*I didn't realise.*

No, I don't suppose you would.

*What's that supposed to mean?*

It's your age – teenagers suffer from a most terrible affliction.

*Yeah, what's that then?*

Self-absorption – you can think only of yourself and your own little world.

*That's quite rude. You're being unfair.*

You would think that – it's part of the affliction. One can't take criticism.

*Look, I realise the screaming's no good. I agree with you on that, it's just I don't know what to do about it.*

My dear, it's all in the mind.

*Yeah, but it's not like we're fully in control. I mean, I don't seem to be able to stop it. It just comes over me after everything else.*

Do you not think we all have something to scream about?

*I've never really thought about it.*

That's exactly what I'm trying to say – self-absorption. It's not your fault. It's your age, the neurological changes and raging hormones – not that they exist for you in the truest sense any more.

*So, what's up with you then?*

I beg your pardon?

*You said everyone has something to scream about. If that's the case, what are you upset about?*

Ah, I have perhaps been a little disingenuous. You see, I have come to terms with all I did or more to the point what I didn't do. I hope it will be the same for you.

*I have no clue what you're talking about.*

I too was left with a certain level of distress, shall we say. I couldn't rest, especially at night. I'm not sure why the night should cause such a problem but I suspect the constant hum of traffic and the general babble of the living somehow acts as a distraction during daylight, while at night the living retire to their beds and quieten and we are left truly alone to face ourselves.

*You're scaring me now.*

I'm sorry, that's not my intention. You see I sense my presence is waning. I'm nearly done and I would very much like to help you as much as I can before I go.

*Go? Lionel, you can't leave. I'll be on my own.*

I don't have a choice, my dear.

*Lionel!*

It's not imminent as far as I know, but you said yourself that my days are numbered. I am one of the senior benches along here – decrepit is the word.

I feel like crying but there are no tears to come out, or nowhere for them to run from. *Do we really exist?* I ask.

I would say we're on another plane at best, one with its own set of rules.

*And they are?*

My dear, you're jumping ahead of yourself. You said there's someone you want to see. This someone is or was your boyfriend – am I correct?

*Yes, he's called Gabriel.*

But, he's in prison charged with your murder?

*He didn't do it.*

And you know who did?

*It wasn't him.*

Yes, but do you know who did it?

*Yeah, I know.*

So, who was it exactly?

I concentrate hard, trying to force the knowledge out, but it's no good.

*I know that I know*, I say, *it's just it's locked inside for some reason.*

Ah, I see, you've blanked out a bad memory, no doubt.

*I think I must have done.*

That's not so helpful.

*I definitely know it wasn't Gabe and I have to get him out, and that's what I've been trying to tell you. I managed to break through.*

Good heavens, really? That's awfully quick.

That guy, the skinny one with the headphones, he definitely heard me sing because he came back with his friend hoping that his friend would also hear me.

And you sang?

*I left it too late. I'm so annoyed with myself. Thing is, I was so amazed he'd heard me that I didn't think. I sang as they were leaving but they must have been too far away. It shows I can do it though. All I need is for someone to sit here today and I can say what I need to say and help free Gabriel.*

This is exceedingly good news, my dear.

The sky brightens and the passers-by increase: workers on their way to the office, dog walkers and parents with their children on the school run.

*Someone has to sit here surely.*

Give it time, Lionel says.

*Why does no one stop?*

My dear, you can see how cold it is. The frost is yet to melt but fear not, people do sit for all sorts of reasons.

*Yes, but look how many benches there are.* Even from my fixed position, not including Lionel, I can count four benches in one direction and nine in the other.

*We're two of fifteen*, I say. *People can choose any one of fifteen benches in this short stretch of riverside path. It's so unfair. No one will ever sit here, not unless they're mad or drunk or a visiting relative.*

Just you wait until summer – people will stop all the time.

*Summer is ages away. I can't wait that long.*

*Please sit here*, I say to each and every person I see.

*Please stop*, I beg the woman with a kid on a scooter, and the man with the fat Jack Russell, and a little old lady with a walking stick.

*You need to take it easy and rest for a while.*

She does stop, but she chooses Lionel.

*No, not there – please just a few more steps.*

I am a decrepit old bench, Lionel says. May I recommend the one next door? It's almost brand new and far more comfortable.

But the lady's short of breath and must rest immediately.

My dear, you can still break through, Lionel says. You must try.

*Hello, madam, sorry to disturb you, but I have an urgent message. Can you hear me? Please nod or say yes.*

The old lady raises one of her legs.

She's taking the weight off her feet, Lionel says. She has a gammy leg.

*She's got a hearing aid. She must be deaf. She'll never hear me.*

Don't worry about that, Lionel says. It is not through the ears that anyone will hear you. Your words have to go straight in. Try again, my dear. Perseverance is key.

*Hello, madam, I hope you're feeling better now that you're sitting down. I'm sorry to disturb you, but I really need to talk to you – to pass on an urgent message. It's about my boyfriend Gabriel Walker. He's the sweetest, loveliest person you could ever meet, he really is. Only he's been accused of something he didn't do. I need – sorry, but can you hear me? Can you hear anything? Please nod or say something? Really, it's so important.*

The old lady looks down as she wiggles her feet, moving each one clockwise and then anticlockwise.

*Please say you can hear me?*

Her breathing steadies. 'Brrr,' she shakes, and buttons up the top of her coat. Using the armrest, she pulls herself up, arranges her walking stick into position.

Sing, Lionel says.

Thinking of an old song that the lady might like, I sing the start of *Oh, What A Beautiful Morning.* She doesn't respond so I think of another show tune that Nanna likes. I sing *Tomorrow* from Annie. I give it my all in a slower, sadder tone.

And yet she shuffles away…

*It didn't work. I don't get it. The young guy with the beard definitely heard me, so why didn't she?*

Perhaps she didn't sit in the right place after all.

*You have no idea how jealous I was when she chose you.*

The old girls still find me attractive, you know – life in the old boy yet.

*Behave, Lionel.*

I apologise, but one does have to amuse oneself.

I sigh. *This is never going to work.*

Don't give up, my dear. Why don't you tell me about your death day?

*Why would I want to do that?*

It's a special day when it's all about you – much like your birthday, but at the other end of your life.

*You go first.*

There's nothing to tell.

*Why's that?*

You know what old people die of?

*Heart attack, stroke … I don't know?*

Boredom.

*You're joking me.*

It's true, although you'll never know what it's like to go into irreversible decline: your body slows up and everything aches, and yet bizarrely you wake up far earlier than you ever have before, making the day stretch out before you – one long hour after another that has to be filled, but you can no longer enjoy a decent walk, your eyesight and hearing are buggered and half your friends are dead.

*Are you serious?*

A woman sits down. I hadn't noticed her approach because I'd been listening to Lionel. She looks about thirty and has long dark hair sticking out beneath a white woolly hat. She pulls a pram up close to the bench, reaches in, and lifts out a baby that's been doubled in size by its padded snowsuit.

The baby's sucking on a dummy and its face is red. Despite the cold, the woman opens her quilted coat, pulls up her jumper, undoes the cup of her bra, pulls out the baby's dummy and before it can wail puts its mouth to her breast.

*That's so embarrassing.* I know it can't be helped but I'd rather look away, like it should be private, but it could be ages until someone else sits here so I'm just going to have to ignore what she's doing and try and break through.

*Hello, thanks for sitting here*, I say. *Don't be scared. I'm not, like, a creepy ghost or anything. My name's Ren – not Lauren like it says on the bench. Your baby's really cute, by the way. I don't normally like babies that much. I always think I'm going to make them cry. You have to look at them the right way, don't you?*

*Can you hear me?*

The woman jiggles her legs up and down. 'Come on, Honey Bear, Mummy's cold, please hurry.' She strokes the baby's cheek.

*It's no good. She can't hear me. Why can't she hear?*

My dear, she's somewhat preoccupied, Lionel says. She may quite simply have too much to do, on top of which she's probably suffering from sleep deprivation and the cold.

*I don't get it, why is it only the skinny bearded man with the headphones who can hear me?*

I couldn't say for sure, but I think some people may be more receptive to the hidden parts of this world than others. An old lady who can barely breathe and has trouble with her feet or a mother coping with the demands of a young baby may not have the ability or space in their lives to open up to what is less obvious.

*I'm just going to keep talking.*

Good idea.

*I'll treat it as practice.*

Atta girl.

*My boyfriend Gabriel, he's the sweetest, loveliest person and he's good with kids. He used to babysit for a woman on his estate. He never charged her much because he knew she was struggling. I used to get upset sometimes because it meant he wasn't always free to see me. This woman worked evenings and I even got suspicious and thought he was cheating on me, but he'd never do that.*

*He really is the kindest, sweetest person and he's beautiful too – if you could see him, you'd agree. He didn't make a big deal of it though; he's not big-headed. He always says it's what's inside that counts. I once said, 'Okay then, would you still love me if I was fat and ugly?' And he said, 'Of course not,' and laughed and laughed until I punched his arm – playfully of course, because I'd never hurt him and he'd never hurt me, whatever anyone says. And that's why I need your help. The police have charged him, put him in jail, and said he did something he'd never do. Gabriel loves me and I love him. Can you hear me? Please help me out? I really need someone to listen.*

Lionel shouts, Sing, Ren, sing.

And, because I think it's unlikely to work, I choose Dusty Springfield's *If You Go Away* and sing it as sad as I can because Gabriel has gone and I'm unable to help, and like the song says, it's as if the sun may as well never ever shine again.

# FOURTEEN

Dusk, and Lionel's gone wherever what remains of Lionel goes, while I watch the water and wait, determined to travel elsewhere, back to when I first met Gabe.

I see him. He's there at Chicken Shack. He looks back, and momentarily our eyes lock. 'Who is he?' Maddy tells me his name and then ruins it by saying, 'He's in a thing with someone', only it turns out he's not. I send him a Facebook friend request and he accepts.

Back to Bourne's on Monday and I look for Gabriel on the bus, but he's not there. Registration: Anders is back on my case and then it's English, which I like, followed by history, which I don't. *Please, Gabriel, be in Chicken Shack.*

Carina, hair fixed and make-up reapplied in the college toilets, opens the door to Chicken Shack and makes straight for the counter. Idris turns and smiles.

'Aw, that's so cute,' I say.

'And yet at the same time – sickening,' Maddy says.

Gabriel Walker does not make an appearance.

*What's the matter with him? Why isn't he here?*

Bus home at the end of the day and still no Gabriel.

Facebook: I have thirty notifications and one message.

Gabriel: 'Hey, Ren – you can sing! Love it'

*What?* I click on notifications – someone (and it has to be Maddy) has uploaded a video of me singing *At Last* from the night she stayed over at mine.

Oh my God, I'm in my tiger onesie and my eyes are shut.

The video has thirty likes and people are liking it all the time – the number goes up by another five in as many seconds – and there are comments:

Kemi: 'Superstar in the making – love you'

Gemma: 'The Voice'

Griff: 'Open your eyes'

*Yeah, thanks for that, you two-timing rat. Must block him.*

Video: 64 likes.

I reply to Gabriel: 'Thanks re singing, but I look stupid with eyes closed. Missed you today – you OK?'

Video: 72 likes.

I call Maddy and tell her to take it down.

'If you insist, but don't blame me in years to come when you've wasted your life in perpetual obscurity.'

The following morning it's still there.

Video: 521 likes. *That must be everyone I know.* And there are even comments from people I don't know such as 'What soul' and 'Beautiful voice'.

And more to the point – a message from Gabriel:

'Been off college, back today – maybe see you x'

*A kiss!*

I arrive early at college and Anders doesn't have a go. *What's going on?* I look down at what I'm wearing: black skirt, tights, Doc Marten shoes and a grey jumper. *Yeah, apart from messy hair, I probably do look employable.*

It's art all morning and while I draw, I put on my headphones and listen to Amy and singers that inspired her: Etta James, Billie Holliday, Dinah Washington, Ella Fitzgerald, Carole King and Sarah Vaughan.

Chicken Shack. I am so ready to go but Carina's in tears. 'I never want to see that place again, let alone eat that crap.'

Maddy makes a face like she thinks Carina has lost it.

'Idris let you down?' I say.

'Why did you say his name? I don't want to hear it ever again.' She runs out. And whatever it is that's going on, I know Chicken Shack ain't happening.

Maddy goes after her and I follow.

'Ren, I've been looking for you.' Holly Appleby stops me and as it's ages since we last spoke, I'm taken aback. 'Your singing's amazeballs,' she says, and all I can think is, *Who says that?*

I say, 'Thanks' and move as if to walk around her towards the toilets and the crisis that's most likely unfolding therein.

'Wait, I haven't finished.' *Is she for real?* 'I don't know if you've heard, but I'm having a party – my eighteenth – it's going to be party of the year.'

I shrug, making out I don't care about the lack of invite. 'Great – lucky.'

'I saw your video on Facebook or whatever. *I love it.*'

'Cheers, thanks.' Again I try to move round her, but she holds my arm.

'You *have* to sing at my party,' she says, and her intensity makes me laugh. 'What's so funny?'

'Sorry, I can't help it sometimes. It's like a nervous reaction I get.'

'Why would you have a nervous reaction?'

'Oh, you know, I get nervous singing in public.'

'You need to get over that,' she says. 'My party will help. I was thinking about a two- or three-song set. What do you know? We can choose the tracks together and give it a run-through.'

'You're winding me up?'

'Ren, *hello*, of course I want you at my party – you're an internet sensation.'

'What?' I make a face, assuming she's taking the piss.

'You've gone viral.' Holly opens Facebook on her phone. The

video has 3,012 likes – more of a small-time internet sensation than a global "Subo" moment but it's certainly more "likes" than anyone else at college has ever had.

I shake my head, incredulous. 'I told Maddy to delete that.' And this time I force my way past her.

'How much d'you want?' Holly shouts after me. 'My dad says I can pay you.'

In the toilets, I find Maddy. 'The video's still online,' I say. 'You promised to delete that.'

'Shush.' She gestures towards the cubicle. Carina has locked herself in and is refusing to come out. Maddy mouths: 'It's over.'

'Carina, you OK in there?' I say. 'How about we take you for coffee somewhere? It'll help. Seriously, Carina, I went out with this right idiot back in Devon,' I say, referring to Griff. 'I'm over it now. It takes a few weeks but you will be OK, I promise.'

Carina blubs, and Maddy rolls her eyes. 'Carina, sod him, he's just a man –they're not worth it – they never are. He's nothing.'

'Bit harsh,' I say.

'She's had a lucky escape – yet another dick – they're all the same,' Maddy says. 'Look, I heard Anders once got the caretaker in to take the door off its hinges when another girl wouldn't come out. She was so embarrassed.'

Again there's silence, until eventually Carina moves the bolt across.

'Finally,' Maddy says, and I give Carina a hug.

Chicken Shack is out so we head to the nearest coffee shop and I buy Carina a large mochaccino in the hope that milky, chocolatey coffee will help.

'This is cold.' Maddy gets up, abruptly scraping her chair back. She returns to the counter. 'This is no good. I want a fresh cup.' She's scowling as she returns. 'They're clueless.'

'At least they replaced it,' I say.

'Too right.' She frowns as she sips at the now scorching coffee.

'I'm sure it was a simple mistake.'

'She's useless. I'd fire her.' She glowers at the barista.

'Wow, don't mess with the Madster,' I say. 'I reckon you'll run a global company one day – such exacting standards – and kind of ruthless.'

Maddy changes the subject. 'Have you heard Holly's sending out invites in batches? The spoilt bitch is playing games – getting people to suck up.'

Carina twists a sachet until it rips and sprays sugar over the table. 'I don't want to go anyway,' she says.

'She wants me to sing.'

'She *what*?' Maddy looks furious, as if this request is a personal affront to her and I can't help laughing. 'What d'you mean sing?'

'She's asked me to sing at her party. I thought she was joking.'

'Holly doesn't do humour,' Maddy says.

'She said she'd pay me.'

Carina's eyes fill with tears. 'I love your singing.'

I give Carina a hug. 'Thanks, but I'd just look stupid. I always close my eyes.'

Maddy sits back. 'Say you'll do it but only if we all get an invite. It'll be party of the year. Her dad's loaded.'

'You said it's going to be shit,' I say.

'I've been to quite a few of her parties,' Carina says.

'What were they like?' I ask.

'She had the most amazing bouncy castle once.'

'What was that – her fifth birthday or something?'

'Must have been.'

'And that was her best party?'

Carina smiles for the first time that day. 'Yeah.'

'See,' Maddy says, 'Holly needs you.' She folds her arms and stares at me, waiting for the only answer she wants to hear. 'I'm not missing out.'

'OK, OK. I'll do it.'

* * *

Bus home and Gabriel's sitting at the back with Aaron.

'Oi, oi,' someone shouts and I assume it's Aaron – *dickhead.*

I have a seat that I give up for an old lady and so once again I'm standing by the exit and Gabriel will have to come close to disembark. My stomach churns.

It's his stop. I feel myself redden and glance back as Gabriel moves down the bus towards the exit, and towards me.

'Go, Gabe,' Aaron shouts.

Gabriel's looking at me. 'Hey,' he says, 'you OK?'

Everything feels too fast as I look into his soft brown eyes and struggle to speak. 'I'm good, thanks, and you?' When what I really want to say is: Let's go out somewhere, I don't care where – anywhere would be good as long as I'm with you.

The bus stops fast and I jolt forward as does everyone else, including Gabriel, who crashes into me. 'Sorry, sorry,' he says. 'You OK?' His hand momentarily touches my lower back. It's the briefest touch and yet that small coat-covered patch of back is on fire.

'Yeah, course,' I say. 'I'm going to Holly's party, by the way.'

He jumps onto the pavement. 'I'll message you.'

And a moment later my phone pings: 'Happy about party – now worth going'

I message back: 'Have to sing – terrified'

Gabe: 'You'll smash it'

Video: 7,203 likes.

Chat messages between Gabriel and me: endless.

Gabriel is now Gabe, we are that close.

Time left until Holly's party: four days.

I practise in my room, including voice exercises to extend my vocal range. (Susannah's idea.) And I even sing for the family.

'I need a drink to relax,' I say, as Nicholas, Susannah, Alicia and Marie all sit around the table and wait for me to start.

'Dream on,' Susannah says.

I stand up, take a deep breath, look around and sit down again.

'*Ren.*' Alicia folds her arms and sits forward, her eyes are wide.

'All right.' I try again, closing my eyes this time; I take myself elsewhere. It's the only way I can do it. *At Last* – my YouTube hit. And I'm away, back in Etta James and Beyoncé-land, losing myself.

'Eyes,' Susannah shouts.

I open them, but look over their heads. It works for me that way. 'D'you think *At Last* is a bit slow for a party?'

Susannah nods. 'Could be a little sophisticated for a teenage party.'

'It works,' Nicholas says, 'go with it.'

Next up is *You Know I'm No Good* – my favourite song and I'm enjoying myself – and finally, I sing *Valerie.*

Alicia's on her feet clapping, and then they all are.

Saturday – video: 14,026 likes.

Skype chat with Gabe: fifty minutes. It ends because his dad calls him.

'Gotta go,' he says, 'see you tonight.'

'I'm shitting myself.'

He smiles. 'Don't do that, whatever you do.'

'I wish it was just a party and I didn't have to sing.'

'You'll be great, don't worry.'

We gaze at one another. I don't want to look away, but his dad shouts again.

Gabe winks. 'Gotta go. See you later.'

I'm left alone, clutching my stomach in the vain hope that'll steady my nerves.

# FIFTEEN

I wear my new dress. It's black and lacy with a gathered skirt, and I backcomb and pin up my hair. It looks way darker than normal due to all the different hair products I've used.

Maddy and Carina arrive to get ready at mine.

'Your room is so beautiful,' Carina says, 'and your own bathroom – I'd love that. You are so lucky.'

Maddy shakes her head. 'Beyond lucky. This place is obscene.'

'The thing is I'm not allowed to put up any posters because of the wallpaper so it doesn't really feel like my room.'

Maddy makes a face. 'Poor you. My heart bleeds.'

'I love the wallpaper,' Carina says. 'It's so romantic. I reckon animals and birds do fall in love. I mean, think of swans – they stick together.'

Maddy shoots me a look, as if she thinks Carina's talk of birds in love will cause her to link to Idris and break down. She changes the subject. 'Are you ready, or what?' Maddy's tapping her foot.

Downstairs, Nicholas is waiting. 'You look like The Ronettes gone punk,' he says, faintly amused by our party dresses, heels and big hair. He's offered us a lift.

'Shall I drop you at the stage entrance?' Nicholas says.

'Bare funny, Dad.' It's the first time I've called him "Dad", and I feel myself redden as he glances over with a beaming smile.

As we approach the venue I spot Holly's boyfriend and his mates standing by a clump of star-shaped helium balloons that are bumping into one another in the breeze. 'That's it. It's there.'

The boat club's a large space on the first floor with a long L-shaped bar and a balcony overlooking the river. There are fairy lights strung around the room and more balloons.

'What's with the wedding music?' I say.

'Saturday night,' Maddy says. 'A decent DJ ain't gonna be doing an eighteenth birthday party at a boat club.'

'See, Holly needs you,' Carina says. 'You'll save the day.'

Lily, a girl I sit with in English comes over, flicking her long dark hair. 'Can't wait to hear you sing.' She's being nice but my stomach flips.

Holly's nearby, surrounded by girlfriends. 'Ren, there you are. I was beginning to think you weren't coming.'

I say, 'Happy birthday,' but it comes out all squeaky and pathetic.

'You're on after the food while Karl, the DJ (hot, isn't he), has a break.'

'Where's Ren's dressing room?' Maddy asks.

'Oh, I didn't think…'

'She's kidding,' I say.

'I'm Ren's manager, didn't she tell you? Now, about the rider…'

'Sorry?'

'She's messing about. I could do with a drink though.'

Maddy passes me a vodka and lemonade and I down it in one and go to the bar to collect another. And even though I know I should pace myself, I can't.

'Your turn to get the drinks in, Carina,' I say.

'I haven't even finished my first one yet.'

'I thought you'd be up for a drink after the Idris thing.'

Maddy scowls. 'Don't remind her.'

'I was feeling good as well,' Carina says. 'All right for you though, isn't it?'

'What?'

'Lover boy,' Maddy says, as she nods towards the door.

*Gabriel.* He looks hot in dark chinos and a shirt and I feel this weird wave of something come over me. 'Give us a swig?' I borrow Carina's glass and knock back more vodka, as Gabriel looks over and holds his hand up to wave.

'Who's he with?' Carina asks.

'You over Idris already?'

'Stop saying that name. I told you. I'm pissed off now.'

Maddy shakes her head. 'Chill out, Carina, seriously. Forget him.'

We all look towards the bar where Gabe's standing.

I go over and he greets me with a smile and introduces his friend Ross.

'I'm Carina.' She's followed me over. It makes me laugh, and better than that, it means she can distract Ross, leaving me to talk to Gabe alone. The music's loud, we can hardly hear each other. I suggest we go outside to the balcony over the river. It's pretty looking out over the water, but there's a cold breeze.

Gabriel sees me shiver and puts his arms around me. 'You OK? You seem cold.'

We huddle together at the far end where it's quieter. 'I like your dress. You look beautiful. What have I said? You are.'

I shake my head. 'Don't – you can't say that.'

'Seriously, you are.'

'*You* look amazing,' I say, and he pushes a strand of hair out of my eyes. I'm right up close, closer than I've ever been. I check out the small flecks of black in his hazel eyes and how there's a darker rim to his iris. And he looks right back and into me. My heart pumps faster, terrified someone will interrupt or Gabe will change his mind. This is all I want. I shiver and he holds me tight. I look up: his soft kind eyes are serious. He means this. I feel his breath and we kiss.

I want to stay there all night but there's a rumbling feeling of dread rising up inside me. People are on the balcony with paper plates piled with food. The buffet's open. I glance at the door where there's a flash of blonde hair and perfect teeth.

'Ren, that's where you're hiding.' Holly gives Gabe a sly smile like she knows exactly what's going on. 'Hurry and grab some food, you're on in five.'

'As if I can eat.'

'You're shakin'.' Gabriel rubs my bare arms, making me fizz inside like his touch is somehow magically charged. 'Let's go inside – can't have a cold superstar.'

'I'm worried about closing my eyes. I can't help it.'

'Don't worry, it's the voice that matters and you've got that.' We step back into the bar area and hang near the back.

'Ren,' Holly ushers me over. She has the microphone. 'Here she is, her video's gone viral, with over 26,000 hits so far. It's our very own internet sensation: Ren Miller.'

There's clapping as far as I can make out, but I'm not sure I'm fully aware. I move automatically. *I have to do this.* There's a hand on my back, someone encouraging me forward. I glance back – it's Gabe. And he smiles, as someone else passes me a microphone. The music starts up, the intro to *At Last* – a song I know inside out. *Don't I?*

I close my eyes, take a deep breath and transport myself elsewhere. The words come out and keep coming as I lose myself and come back again. *Open your eyes.*

There are so many people: sitting and standing, swaying and singing along. Mostly they look at me, though some are turned away at the bar or talking.

*Look over their heads, squint a little, fuzz them out.*

*You Know I'm No Good* – my favourite song.

I look at Gabe and he nods like he's encouraging me. Love you, I think.

*Valerie* – I go for it and people dance. Loads of people get up and I can't believe it. The dance floor's packed and I'm smiling inside as I sing.

And I did it. I sang the lot – reached the end of my set. And there's applause.

People are smiling. There are whistles and whoops.

Maddy rushes over and grabs my arm like she's holding me up. 'That was amazing. I filmed it all.'

'You didn't? Not again, I swear my eyes were closed.'

She shrugs. 'You opened them briefly.'

'I need a drink.'

'Let's dance first,' Maddy says. 'I love this song.'

'Where's Gabe?'

She shrugs. 'He's around somewhere. Come on, dance.'

And I do briefly, but it's a song I hate. 'I can't hack this crap.' I stop and, stony-faced, Maddy abruptly turns away towards the others, while I feel a gentle stroke down my back that sends a wave of warmth and excitement right through me.

# SIXTEEN

*Gabriel: how he touched my face, the loving look he gave as he held me and we kissed* – I can't stop thinking about him. I'm up late, my head a little heavy and with a desperate thirst. In my tiger onesie I go downstairs and my head pounds at the sound of Alicia and her damn cello. 'D'you have to?' I say, as I peer into the Blue Room, where she's sat bolt upright behind her huge beast of an instrument, while visible through the windows are the dogs, barking as they circle the lake.

'*Ren*, come and sing while I play?'

'I've got a headache and you're making it worse.' I go down to the kitchen where Nicholas is listening to some ancient music as he chops cabbage.

'What is that gloomy music?' I say, as I rub my sore head.

'*Don't You Forget About Me*, Simple Minds, best band in the world.'

'Never heard of them. What are you doing?'

'I'm chef today.'

'How come?'

'Marie's off and Susannah's studying. She has an essay due in tomorrow.'

'How can she work with Alicia murdering that cello?'

Nicholas points upwards with the knife he's using. 'She's on the top floor.'

I pour a large glass of orange juice. 'What you cooking?'

'Roast beef, Yorkshire pudding, roast potatoes – the works.'

'Will Susannah eat that?' I sort a bowl of granola with milk and sit at the breakfast bar.

'She will today. How was the party?'

'Good.'

'And the singing? How did it go?'

'OK, I think.'

'Is it on YouTube?'

'Hope not – my eyes were shut.'

'You got a hangover?'

'Not really.' I rub my forehead.

'Are you getting dressed? It's not *The Tiger Who Came to Tea*, you know.'

I roll my eyes. 'You're too funny.' I smile, as I pour a glass of water and return to my room.

Gabriel has football first thing (which is annoying), but I message him anyway: 'Hey, Gabe, you OK? Ren xx.'

Black leggings, stripy monochrome T-shirt and black baggy jumper, and I apply thick black eyeliner with corner flicks. Restless, I go to the window and look down at the drive, the locked gate and beyond where the houses spread out, intercut by a patch of green land and the curving sweep of the river. I want to be out there, anywhere, as long as I'm with Gabe.

Finally, my phone pings.

'Finished footie. You free? Gabe xx.'

By the time we meet up it's nearly dark. Gabriel's waiting outside Poundland. He waves and runs across, dodging through a slow stream of traffic.

At the Sun Café, a small cabin on a terrace above the river, we order cappuccinos and sit by the window and talk about everything from singing to football, his mates, my friends, college, music (he has no taste) and family – he lives with his dad, his mum left years ago.

'She went off with someone else,' he says.

'You see her though?'

'Not any more. There was too much beef with her new man, and she drinks. Her life's chaotic. My dad says their backgrounds were too different. He's from Trinidad and his family are religious and strict, while my mum was brought up in London.'

'She went off with someone else – that's tough.'

He nods. 'What about your folks?'

'My mum's in Devon.'

'How come you don't live with her?'

'I did until recently, but I wanted to get to know my dad.' I don't mention Griff and Izzy and the gross mobile phone footage that burned to such a degree I flipped out and ran away.

'Lucky for me you came to London to meet your dad,' Gabe says. 'What's he like?'

I shrug. 'I don't see a lot of him. He leaves for the City long before anyone else gets up and comes home late, and even when he's back, he's out cycling.'

'Sounds all right. I'd prefer it that way. My old man's always on my case.'

'D'you look like him?' I try to imagine an older Gabriel.

'People say we look alike. I'm lighter skinned and my dad says that'll help with my career.'

'You're clever. You'll be fine.'

'I've got a good memory – not sure that'll get me a job.'

I want to stay and talk all day and night, but I can't. I check my phone. 'I need to get back.'

Gabe offers to walk me home.

'I'll be OK,' I say, not wanting to put him out.

'I want to come – make sure you're OK.'

'It's quite a way. We'll get the bus, yeah?'

'No, let's walk. We can hang for longer.' He smiles – a dimple on one side. He takes my hand and holds it within his. And I love that he does that. We follow the river past a park, along the towpath and I feel lighter, like I've been lifted to another realm where only good things happen. It's like when I'm with Gabe I feel invincible. Hand in hand, we walk over the bridge and along the other side. We pass riverside houses and boatsheds converted into flats and cross a field. While normally I'd moan about such a long walk, with Gabe I can walk forever.

I lead the way down a shortcut through a small alleyway behind several large houses. 'Nearly there,' I say, and Gabriel breaks away and runs ahead.

'What are you doing?'

He launches himself into a backflip.

'You're such a show-off.'

He stops and pulls himself up onto a small tree to peer over a wall. 'That's sick – what a house – take a look.'

'You can't do that.'

'Come on, you gotta see.'

I climb up and peek over. There's a giant white sugar cube of a house with a modern garden designed in a grid with boxed hedging and a central sculpture. 'Looks like a rusting globe.'

'It looks like it's from a shipwreck or something,' Gabe says. 'Let's go in.'

'No way, are you crazy? They're neighbours.'

'What?' He freezes. 'Are you winding me up?' He has a look, one I recognise – a sudden and absolute acknowledgement that our lives are different.

I shrug, not wanting to alienate him in any way. 'I don't live far – a few doors down.'

'Are you for real?' He climbs down and we continue on, until we reach the wide wooden gate of Ambrose House that is, as always, shut.

I key in the code, and Gabriel takes a step back.

'I'm gonna go now.'

'Why? Come in, they're all right.'

'I've got to get back.'

'What for?'

'Stuff to do.'

'Like what?'

'College stuff.'

'It can wait half an hour, can't it? Just say hello and then it's done.'

'My dad's expecting me.'

'He won't mind you staying five minutes more. What is it? What's up?'

'Nothing.' He shakes his head.

'Why won't you come in?'

'I need to get going.'

'Don't go.' I have to stop myself grabbing him.

'I've got to get back.' He kisses me too quickly and it confuses me. 'I'll see you tomorrow,' he says. *Does he mean it?*

I want to keep him there, but can't think how and I'm almost kicking myself as I watch him walk back up the lane.

Back inside, the dogs greet me in the hall as Susannah comes downstairs. 'How was your afternoon?' she says.

'Good, thanks,' I say, even though I'm unsure if it ended well or not.

The Hummingbird Suite isn't really me, I think as I slump onto the floor by my bed. I receive a text on my phone from Gabriel: 'Soz, had to go. Skype later xxx'.

I exhale. It's OK. We're OK: we'll Skype, we'll message, we'll Snapchat and Facetime and I'll see him on the bus, at Chicken Shack and after college.

Facebook: a new video's been uploaded from Holly's party: 'Ren sings again'. I click on "play" – my eyes remain closed, until a moment near the end.

Likes: 33. *Is that all?*

Morning bus: no Gabriel.

Chicken Shack: no Gabriel.

I push my bucket of chicken aside.

'What's happened to the boyfriend?' Maddy asks.

'He's got a lot on today.' I try to sound carefree.

'You fallen out already?'

It irritates me that she thinks that and I shrug, and say, 'We'll catch up later.'

Carina glances at Idris. 'You've got to watch it when they go quiet – make sure there's no one else.' Idris had been seen with another girl, although he claims it was a misunderstanding and he and Carina are texting again.

'Are we still on for Camden Saturday?' Maddy asks.

'Yeah, course.'

'Who's coming?'

'Gabriel –.'

Maddy groans. 'You better not ditch me.' She gives me a look. 'Who else?'

'Aaron, I'm afraid, and Fenton and Ross.'

'Ross?' Carina's face brightens.

'Thought you were back into Idris?'

'Maybe –.'

'And he's bringing James.'

'James?' Maddy says.

'You like him, don't you?'

Maddy shrugs. 'He's OK.'

'Oh, and Lily's coming too.'

'Why's she coming?' Maddy says.

'She heard me talking about it in English and asked if she could come.'

'You sit with her in economics, don't you?' Carina says.

Maddy makes a face. 'She's dull.'

'Fenton and James like her,' I say, as I realise that may be Maddy's problem. Anyhow, whatever, I live for the weekend. Apart from a daily fix of messaging, Gabriel's unavailable. He's studying and helping his dad and then there's football practice and a match on Thursday. I'm not his first priority and that's raw, but then again, he's a challenge.

Saturday, Gabriel has yet another football match. I offer to wait for him but he insists I go ahead with the others, so I head over to Maddy's.

Her mum lets me in. Mrs Costa's chunky with dark wavy hair. She wears loose linen shirts over trousers and flat shoes. 'I've been watching your singing videos,' she says. 'You have many fans.'

'Well, about 30,000 people have watched – what they think, I don't know.'

'You will be great success.' Mrs Costa and her husband are originally from Greece. Maddy said they arrived decades ago and built up their own furniture business. Maddy says her parents work all the time, even though they no longer need to – 'They don't trust anyone,' she says.

'Go on up, Ren – she should be ready for you.'

Even though the house has large windows, it feels gloomy due to the half-closed curtains and old dark furniture.

Upstairs, I knock on Maddy's door. 'Madster, it's me, you in there?'

Maddy's halfway through applying eyeliner. 'You've been talking to my Mum? Ignore everything – she's so embarrassing. Sit there.' She points at her knackered beanbag.

'I swear you've got OCD.' Everything in her room is arranged precisely. The make-up's in pots, her books are neatly stacked and her desk is clear.

'It's called being organised, not something you know about.'

'Yeah, well, you're making us late – so not that organised then.'

We meet the others at the station: Carina, Lily, Aaron, Fenton, Ross and James and catch the train to Camden where we browse the stalls and drink bubble tea at a café in the market, until finally it's time for me to go and meet Gabe. 'I won't be long.' I get up to leave.

'We'll come with you,' Maddy says.

'Nah, stay here and chill.' I try to sound relaxed.

'No, really, we'll come. I'm bored anyway,' Maddy says.

'He could be late, best I go alone.'

Aaron pulls a face, as he glances at a man with various piercings and tattoos on his face. 'You leaving us with the wackos?'

'You fit in fine.' I walk away then, as quickly as I can because more than anything I want time alone with Gabe.

After a few minutes, I spot him coming through the ticket barrier at Camden Town tube station. He looks buff. Every time I see him he looks even better than I remember. I call out, 'Gabe.'

It's like a punch that I didn't see coming. Winded and shocked, I'm knocked out of my nightly reliving as someone sits on the bench.

It's an old man: short, tubby and layered with clothes. He has a straggly beard, long fingernails and a leg that's swollen in shape like an elephant's foot.

The wood of the bench contains me once again and I didn't even reach the moment at Camden Town tube station when Gabe looks up and smiles, so obviously pleased to see me. Couldn't the old man have waited and interrupted me further on?

The old man shifts on the seat, grunts, gets up and delves inside one of those pull-along shopping trolleys that old ladies use. It's kind of a cool one though, in a retro Fifties-style fabric printed with jazzy red apples.

He pulls out a can of what I assume is something strong, bought to keep out the cold or the ability to notice the cold. It must be the sort of minus temperature that can creep right into your bones and take hold.

*You'll be dead alongside me if you stay here all night.*

He grunts again and takes a large, long swig.

*He didn't hear me*, I tell Lionel, but it's too late for Lionel. He won't respond.

I should practise, I think – try and break through. *My name's Ren*, I shout, worried he could be deaf as well as drunk.

He takes another slug of lager or whatever it is, balances the can on the bench and stands up. I can see the can clearly now. It's lemonade – that's all.

And he's back at the shopping trolley, trying to pull out a sleeping bag, but he's clumsy and knocks the can. 'Watch it,' he says. 'I told ye abou' tha'.'

*Sorry*, I say, *are you talking to me?*

'I said, "Watch it, while I sort the bed." '

*Can you hear me?* I feel lightness, as if hope has re-entered my living death.

'Will you hold on there?' He flips back the flap of the trolley.

*You can hear me? My name's Ren – please nod to show you understand?*

'Why are ye askin' me this rubbish? I told ye before. Ye know the score.'

*I just need to know whether or not you can hear me? It's really important, or I wouldn't ask.*

His brow is low, his expression severe. 'Gimme some space. I cannae stand ye hanging round me like a bad smell.'

*Hello, sir, excuse me, sorry to interrupt, but can you hear me?*

'We called it a day back in Glesgae, did we no'?' He shouts at the air to the left of him, his face contorted like a vicious dog.

*There must be some mistake*, I say, *I've never been to Glasgow.*

'It both began and ended in Glesgae. No one invi'ed ye here.' He hits out at the air. 'You're no' welcome.'

He's talking to himself. He must hear voices and has most probably got my voice muddled up with the usual companions or enemies he hears in his head.

*Gabe, I'm sorry, I thought this was it. I thought I could break through. I will though, don't you worry. I'll do it as soon as I can. I'll get you out of that prison hellhole somehow, I promise.*

The old beardy man turns to his left and stares into the darkness. 'What is this?' He shouts, 'Since when did ye bring a lady?'

He *can* hear me, I think. He *can* hear me, but he doesn't understand.

*Hello, can you help me, please? I need someone to listen. Please.*

'Help yer bloomin' self, woman. What d'ye think this is, eh? Who do ye think ye are?' He leans on his trolley, takes another swig of lemonade, drops the can to the ground and staggers away, a lumbering heap trailing his apple-patterned shopping trolley as he shouts in the dark. 'Don't follow me. I cannae stand ye followin' me. I don't need company. I told ye tha' before and now wha' d'ye go and do? Ye bring a lady!'

# SEVENTEEN

A small patrol boat, with "Port of London" written on its side, passes by and seagulls fly above. The sky is white, the river brown, and the path's a damp dark grey, the frost having melted.

*I must be getting old*, I tell Lionel.

And why is that, pray tell?

*The day's dragging like you said it does when you're old.*

We can but talk and entertain ourselves.

*We're stuck in the past, aren't we?*

A cyclist in a fluorescent yellow jacket flits by.

Your past is new to me. I'd love to hear more.

*I'd rather hear about you and your life.*

My dear, imagine you've been here so long that your wood is covered in a film of greenish mould that is eating you away.

*You say some bare revolting things sometimes.*

The bench is nothing to me.

*What did you do?*

In life, do you mean?

*Yeah.*

I was retired.

*What, all your life? I don't think so.*

The thing about retirement is that you almost forget what came before.

*D'you not want to say or something?*

I ran a bakery.

*Oh, right.*

You are somewhat underwhelmed.

*It's not what I expected.*

What did you expect?

*No offence, but something more gentlemanly or glamorous even.*

Such as?

*I imagined you running a men's clothes shop or a restaurant.*

Ah, well, you're not far off with the latter. I inherited a small bakery, which I built up and extended until I had a shop, tearoom and function room. We catered for christenings, birthdays, bar mitzvahs, weddings and wakes, as well as delivering our baked goods throughout west London. It was a good little business.

*You married?*

Yes, to Isobel.

*Where did you meet?*

At the Café de Paris, near Piccadilly in London, 1940.

*That is so long ago.*

Yes, it *so* is.

*What was the Café de Paris like?*

Wonderful – sweeping staircases, chandeliers, velvet sofas and a circular dance floor. They had a live band in those days and the girls – everyone dressed up: fabulous dresses, hair curled, red lipstick and heels. Isobel was the prettiest girl there. And to think it was bombed a year later.

*I guess it's not there any more.*

I'm sure it is. They rebuilt it after the war.

*Were you in the army during the war?*

No, baker was a reserved occupation. London needed bread.

*I hadn't thought of that.*

A small child is at the bench. He looks about three and is wearing a woolly hat and parka. He taps the wooden slats. 'Look, Mummy, a bear.' He lifts the little white bear with a red heart on its belly that my mum stuck in the corner.

'Put it back, sweetheart,' his mother says. She's dressed older than she looks in a fitted red coat and black knee-high leather boots.

'But it's lost.'

'I think it's meant to be there.'

'It's wet.'

*Take it,* I say. *You can have it. The bear wants to go home with you.*

'The bear wants to come, Mummy.'

'Darling, put it back. Someone's put it there especially.'

'Why?'

'This bench is for a special girl who died.' The woman's eyes glisten. 'She was seventeen years old. That may sound old to you, but it's actually quite young, so her mummy and daddy have put a little bear there to keep her company.'

*Your mum seems very nice,* I say, *but she's wrong. Seventeen is, like, practically an adult. I am way too old for cuddly toys. I'd much rather you looked after the bear. Please take him, thank you.*

'She wants me to take him.'

'We can't take him, sweetie. He belongs here.'

*Please take the bear. I don't want him.*

The boy grips the bear.

'Give me the bear, Thomas.'

'No, it's mine – she said.'

'It belongs here, Thomas. I just explained that.'

*Take it, take the bear, but tell your Mummy I need her help. There's a boy called Gabriel Walker. He's in prison for something he didn't do. Tell your mum to Google Gabriel Walker.*

'It's Gabriel.'

'What – you've called the bear Gabriel?'

'Gabriel...'

*Your mum needs to Google Gabriel Walker.*

'You mean the Christmas story,' his mum says. 'Do you remember learning about it at nursery? The angel Gabriel appeared to Mary and told her she was going to have a baby. You remember the Christmas play at nursery? You were a sheep and who was it – your friend Dylan? He was dressed up as the angel Gabriel, wasn't he?'

*No, that's not it, Thomas. Your mum's not listening. Tell her the bench is for a girl called Lauren. Say that: the bench is for Lauren.*

'The bench – Lauren.'

'What's that?' His mother stares at him, and then looks back at the plaque. She pales and a deep crease furrows her brow. 'How do you know that?'

'She said.'

'What do you mean?'

'She said I can have the bear.'

'Tommy, I'm being serious now, did you hear something?'

'Can you help? She's lost her friend.'

The woman snatches the bear from his podgy hand and throws it back onto the bench. 'We're going.'

'She said I can have it.'

*Gabriel, Gabriel Walker – please say the name – tell your mum, it's Gabriel.*

His face crumples as she pulls him away and he cries and looks back as she marches him towards the bridge.

You're breaking through, Lionel says. There's no doubt about that.

*Yeah, but it's only mad old men and toddlers that hear me – no one who can actually help. Total fail. Unbelievable.*

It's only a matter of time, my dear. You can do it. One must keep the faith.

*Stupid bear.* I will it to fall off the bench sideways and rot into the earth.

# EIGHTEEN

Alicia runs towards me. She has a large bouquet of black flowers which she holds in front of the plaque as if she thinks it has eyes.

'Aren't they awesome?' she says, a little out of breath. The dogs are at my legs. 'Don't wee there.' Alicia shoves Max away.

Susannah's next and, oh no, my dad's brought Judy.

*All I need*, I say, which makes Lionel stir.

Who's the lady in the fur hat? he asks.

*That's my so-called grandmother, Judy. She's a total bitch. I don't get why she's here. I've only met her once.*

Everybody likes to inspect a bench, and know where it is, et cetera – it's a talking point. She looks rather refined. Why don't you like her?

I think back to the one and only day we met. Sparrow-thin, her golden hair twisted into a fancy chignon, and dressed in a Chanel jacket and skirt, she looked like an ageing film star, as she does now. *She used to be a ballerina*, I tell Lionel. *She still has the figure, and to be honest that alone is enough to piss me off. And she's quite theatrical.*

When she first saw me, she goes, 'Ah, here she is – my first grandchild. Lauren Bethany Miller, we meet at last.'

I went red and said, 'My name's Ren, that's what I like.'

'You have the Miller nose. That's fortunate.' She studied my face and then looked me over. 'Do you dance?'

'What, like classes you mean?'

'Yes – ballet, tap, modern?'

I told her I'd never done any dance classes. Mum couldn't afford any extra activities, though I didn't mention that. And she said it was a shame I hadn't as "it helps". And that made me feel bad and maybe Susannah realised because she said, 'Ren likes singing – she has a great voice although she's a little shy about it.'

Judy shook her head. 'Shyness never helped anyone. If you have a talent, you must let everyone know. One does not get to dance with Rudolf Nureyev through being shy.' She then knocked back another tumbler of whisky though she only picked at the meal Susannah cooked.

I asked my grandmother if she lived in Putney, as I knew that was where my dad was brought up.

'No, I prefer zone one,' she said. "Zone one" didn't mean anything to me back then as I'd only been in London a week. And I must have looked confused because she explained, 'Zone one – central London. I live in Chelsea, off the King's Road.'

'Mother likes going out – fine dining and the latest shows,' Nicholas said.

'I have a wonderful time with my many dear friends and of course no one ever dies in Chelsea. We have the longest life expectancy in the whole of the UK, so you're all going to have to put up with me a good while longer.'

'And Mr Miller, my grandad?' I asked.

Judy looked away as if she were searching for him. 'Cancer, pancreatic, three years ago – we only had a few weeks post-diagnosis.'

'I'm sorry.'

Judy gave a small nod.

'Did he live in Chelsea?' The question slipped out without thinking. And there was a moment's silence before Judy roared with laughter.

'Yes, yes, he did,' she said, wiping at her eyes with a cotton handkerchief.

* * *

Lionel chuckles, and I'm back to watching my family mill around me on the riverside. At least your grandmother has a sense of humour, she can't be all bad, he says.

Alicia's at the bench, fussing over the flowers. 'Where shall I put them?' She tries them on one side, and then moves them. 'The bear wants to be near the flowers. They could act as an umbrella and keep him dry.'

'It's a bit late for that, my darling.' Judy pokes at the soggy bear and even though I hate the bear, it annoys me that she's being rude about it.

'Put them wherever you think's best,' Susannah says.

'Someone's moved this bear,' Alicia says. 'It was in the corner before.'

*I don't care about the bear*, I say.

Alicia stares at the bear. 'Don't you like the bear, Mummy?'

'What's that, darling?'

'The bear – why don't you like it?'

'I do like it, it's sweet.'

'I think it's ghastly,' Judy says. 'You spend good money on a quality bench and someone adds cheap tat – who on earth put that there?'

'It may have been Lauren's mum,' Susannah says.

'Oh, yes, what's her name?' Judy says.

*Annie, that's my mum's name, and Susannah, why are you calling me Lauren?*

'I like Annie,' Alicia says, and I wonder if she's responding to me or Judy.

'What are those flowers?' Dad says.

'They're black for Ren,' Alicia says. 'She liked black.'

'You would not believe the effort I had to go to find black flowers in February,' Susannah says.

*Did you hear that, Lionel? It's February. It must be 2013.*

February, well I never, Lionel says. We're back in touch and fully aware.

'Of course, no flowers are truly black,' Judy says. 'They're either very dark purple or the deepest red.'

'They look good like that, Alicia, well done,' Dad says. 'Right, let's go and eat.' He taps the top of the bench as if he's patting one of the dogs.

*Hold on*, I say, *we need to talk. Please – you must listen.*

Dad shuffles on the spot as if he's cold.

'I'm not going yet.' Alicia sits down and folds her arms.

'Alicia, the bench is damp,' Judy says. 'You'll ruin your coat.'

'I want to be as close to Ren as possible.'

'I'm sure she knows you're here, sweetheart.'

'She does.' Alicia grips the edge of the seat.

*Alicia, you can hear me?*

Alicia folds her arms and pouts. 'It's not right that we're going away without Ren.'

Nicholas squeezes her shoulder. 'Ren would want you to go on having fun, you know that. And besides, she probably wouldn't have wanted to go skiing with us anyway. She always preferred to be with her friends.'

'That was the problem, ultimately,' Susannah says.

*You're not wrong*, I say, *but I never got to go skiing. I would've been up for giving it a go. Why not?*

'She would go,' Alicia says. 'If I asked her, she'd go.'

'You two were very close,' Susannah says, 'there's no doubt about that.'

*Alicia, can you hear me?* I say. *Push the dogs away. They're really annoying me.*

Alicia jumps up. 'George, Max, show some respect.' She shoos them away.

*You can hear me. Listen, this is important. It wasn't Gabriel. He never hurt me. He never would. He's not like that.*

Alicia freezes in front of the bench. Her eyes are wide.

*Alicia, please believe me.*

Her mouth creases at the corners as she tries to hold it together.

'Are you OK, sweetheart?' Susannah says.

Nicholas pulls Alicia's hat down over her eyes.

'Stop it, Daddy.' She hits out. 'I want to go now.'

'Good, I'm starving,' Nicholas says. 'Let's find a restaurant.'

'*Is there* anywhere decent to eat around here?' Judy says.

'It'll have to be a pub meal,' Susannah says. 'Most places don't allow dogs.'

'You can't discuss food in front of Ren. It's not fair.'

'Ren can't hear what we're saying,' Judy says.

'She never listened to me anyhow,' Nicholas says.

'How do you know she can't hear you?' Alicia says.

Susannah puts her arm around Alicia and says, 'I know it's hard but we all have to accept she's gone. Let's go and eat. We'll be back here on Wednesday anyhow.'

'Why?'

'It's the memorial service,' Nicholas says. 'Have you forgotten already?'

'We're coming here afterwards,' Susannah says.

'I hear you'll be saying a few words,' Judy says. 'That's very brave. I'm extremely proud of you.'

They walk away, with Alicia intermittently glancing backwards with a fearful look in her eye.

*She heard me.*

# NINETEEN

I long for dusk. *Nothing feels right today*, I tell Lionel.

Why is that, my dear?

*I think it's because I was interrupted last night when the homeless man sat on the bench. It halted what was happening. I didn't get to replay everything and it's like important moments are missing.*

Those moments did occur; you do realise that? Your life is complete.

*I know, but it's like I have to replay it all every night, and having been interrupted, it's as if I've left Gabriel in limbo, stuck at the ticket barrier in Camden Town Tube station.*

It's a curious thing this endless reliving. Perhaps your mind (or what's left of it) is trying to work out what happened.

*I know what happened.*

Yes, but do you understand it?

*I'm not sure it is understandable.*

That could well be the case. Some events are completely nonsensical.

*I guess there must be some sort of reason why it all keeps replaying the way it does.*

You weren't prepared to leave.

I think back and lose myself in that moment.

*Gabriel was shouting – calling out to me – although he must have been too far away for me to hear. It was all in my head, wasn't it?*

I'm sure that he *was* shouting your name and that you somehow knew that.

*What about you – why did you stay?*

It was Janet, my daughter.

*You needed to see her again?*

I wanted to apologise.

*Why?*

My dear, as you can see, the lamps have been lit, and the night is drawing in, so I'll not start this now. Goodnight, Ren, rest in peace – not that you will, but I like to say it anyway. Rest in peace.

*Goodnight, Lionel, rest in peace.*

As a fox skulks the undergrowth and the moonlit river flows, I leave the riverside and am once again at Bourne's, first day, heading to Chicken Shack with Maddy and Carina. We buy our meal deals and sit on the left-hand side. Four fit lads walk in; Maddy and Carina look at one another and turn around at the perfect moment to say, "All right". And there he is, last one in, *Gabriel.* And I feel it all again, an incredible rush as we hold each other's gaze – until Maddy tells me 'He's in a thing with someone' and I look down at my food to hide my disappointment.

Back at Ambrose House, I listen to Amy Winehouse's *Love Is A Losing Game* on repeat, until I check Facebook and realise that Maddy's wrong – Gabriel Walker's not 'in a thing' with anyone. It's back on and I see him on the bus and I see him at Chicken Shack. He likes me and I like him. It should be easy, but it isn't. Via Facebook I send a 'friend request' and after some delay (he's not that into Facebook) he accepts and we message one another daily until finally at Holly's party we kiss and it's the best kiss, good enough to cancel out anything that went before – including bitter feelings caused by that rat Griff.

We hang out at the Sun Café and Gabe walks me home. A week later, we meet in Camden at the tube station. Catching sight of him at the ticket barrier, I again can't quite believe how beautiful he is – that perfect face, those eyes, and that lean, fit body.

'Gabe,' I call out, and he looks up and smiles.

'Couldn't be arsed with football today,' he says.

'Yeah, right.'

'No, really, I just want to be with you.'

'You are so lying.'

He laughs. 'Where are the others?'

'They're at a café in the market.'

'We'll meet them later, yeah?' He takes my hand. 'There's something I want to show you.' We turn left out of the station, left again and cross a couple of roads. 'This should be Camden Road.' He checks the street sign. It's busy, people are shouting, a police siren's sounding and there's a scary-looking dog on a rope that I swerve to avoid.

'Looks simpler on the map,' he says.

'Where are you taking me?'

'You'll see.'

We walk for ages, hand in hand, past shops, houses, a supermarket and under a railway bridge, until eventually we take a right-hand turn. 'This is it. We're here.'

The houses are large, white, three or four storeys high with basements: 'Camden Square, NW1 – I know this place.' I do a complete 360. The square's quiet although there are loads of parked cars. I look for a pile of flowers, messages and empty vodka bottles like I saw on the news, but it was a while ago now and it must have been cleared away.

'You're OK with this?' Gabriel says. 'I thought you'd be interested.'

'It's just not how I imagined.'

A man with a shaved head stares before checking a bin. And then I notice a tree that's decorated with cards, ribbons and photos. 'There *is* a shrine.'

The tree has a thick pale trunk that contrasts with the brightly coloured cards and photos that have been stuck to it. There's a black and white photo of Amy Winehouse with her signature black beehive and thick eyeliner that says "Gone too soon", while a floral card says, "Your problems were the same as mine. Lucky for me I don't have your money, RIP". And attached to a shrivelled rose in cellophane: "You gave the world so much. Wish you'd stuck around for more."

There's a lump in my throat and Gabriel hugs me. 'Which house do you think was hers?' I say, biting my lip.

'It's got to be that one.' Gabriel points across the street to a large white townhouse with big black gates.

'That's where she died.'

Gabriel shakes his head. 'She was a genius.'

I love that we agree on Amy, because the rest of the music he likes does nothing for me. 'I wish I had a card or something.' I search through my bag and find only a till receipt for Poundland of all places – hardly rock 'n' roll, but I write on the back of it anyway: "Amy, hope to one day be as good a singer as you. So sad you've gone, your fan forever, Ren xxx". I push it into a gnarly bit of the tree but it won't stick, so I fold it in half and wedge it behind another card.

'What did you write?'

'Not telling you – it's for Amy and no one else.' Gabe gives a small nod like he understands. And I take a photo on my phone of the tree and Amy's house. 'I've got a song going around my head.' I sing the first few lines of *What A Diff'rence A Day Makes.*

'I like that.'

'It's Dinah Washington – one of Amy's favourites.' I take a deep breath and glance around at the parked cars, in the hope that looking at something boring will calm my emotions because I can't help thinking of her and her dad and how close they were, and what he's lost, and what I've barely had.

'Are you OK?' Gabe draws me close. 'Maybe I shouldn't have brought you here.'

'No, I'm glad. I wanted to come when she died, but it's too far from Devon.'

He hugs me, and says, 'She passed way too early.'

The man with the shaved head approaches.

'I don't like the look of him. We should go.'

Gabriel squeezes my hand. 'Yeah, meet the others.'

'Wish we could have stayed longer though,' I say, as we turn back onto Camden Road. 'What if some part of Amy's still there, like her spirit remains or something?'

'What, like she's a ghost?'

'There could be some essence of Amy that somehow lingers.'

'You die and that's it,' he says. 'Amy Winehouse ain't no ghost.'

'Yeah, how sure are you about that? Look, it's a sign.' I point at a wall on the left by a shop, where there's a spray-painted Amy in black with the iconic beehive and a Fifties-style dress. She has wings like an angel or someone who drinks Red Bull. "Pegasus" is the signature. Again I take a photo, and this time I upload it to Facebook.

'That's the Dublin Castle.' I point out a traditional-style pub. 'Amy drank there – she used to hog the jukebox and sometimes serve behind the bar. '

'You're gettin' like me with the facts.'

'Only Amy facts – that's all I know.'

Camden High Street follows with a right turn into Castlehaven Road to check The Hawley Arms – another of Amy's favourites and the pub that had a serious fire that Amy referred to when she collected a Grammy: 'Camden Town ain't burning down.'

"Amy Winehouse is Camden Town" is someone's spray-painted addition to the Camden sign by the lock.

'This place is for freaks,' Gabriel says, as we pass a girl with blue dreadlocks tied in high bunches, alongside her friend who has stacked creepers. And there's a cross-dresser, steampunks, emos and indie kids.

'These are my people.' It's a buzz to be there with the sort of people I want to know and in the place I'd most like to be, one day gigging as Amy did. This is my destiny.

I pause at a tattoo parlour, pulling Gabe over to the window to look at the designs: fish, flowers, clouds, crosses, oriental symbols and skeletons.

'Let's go in.' I push the door.

Inside there's a tall man with spiky hair and tattooed sleeves of flowers in a folk-art style, interspersed with the words "HAPPINESS" and "LOVE". 'Can I help you?' he says.

'I just saw this graffiti of Amy Winehouse with wings. Have you seen it?' He nods. 'Can you do that on my ankle?'

He tilts his chin upwards. 'I could do it. I can do anything – my own version that is. I won't plagiarise another artist, know what I mean? But it all comes down to whether or not you have the correct ID on you?'

'Sure. How much will it cost?'

'Let's see the ID and I'll quote you on it.'

I pass him my student card.

'It's got to be a driving licence or passport,' he says.

'But it's got my photo.'

'It's too easy to fake, sorry.'

'But it's real.'

'Can't risk it. I'd lose my licence.'

'But I've already got a tattoo.'

Gabriel nods. 'She wouldn't have that unless she was eighteen.'

The man shakes his head. 'Like anything there are unscrupulous tattoo artists out there, although I wouldn't call them "artists".'

My phone goes and I consider ignoring it, but it's more trouble than it's worth. 'Ren, it's Susannah. Where are you?'

'London.'

'London, where?'

'Camden.'

'What on earth are you doing all the way up there?'

'Just hanging.'

'I can't believe you've gone there without telling me. Who are you with?'

'Gabriel.'

'What are you doing?'

'Shopping.'

'I want you back by four.'

'Are you serious?'

'I don't want you there after dark.'

'What d'you think's going to happen?'

'You're my responsibility and Camden worries me.'

'Susannah, I'm old enough to look after myself.'

The tattooist folds his arms and gives me one of those looks that say you are so busted. I turn off my phone.

'What time did she say?' asks Gabe.

'Whenever I like.' I lie. 'I'll pop back with my driving licence, yeah,' I say to the tattooist.

'I look forward to it – Amy-with-wings.'

Back at the market, we weave between the stalls selling printed T-shirts, leather bags, and Japanese novelties and find the café where the others are sitting by the entrance, like they're cool enough to attract further customers.

'Gabe, have a toke, mate?' Aaron's smoking shisha.

'You're all right. I'll pass.'

'Come on, don't be a pussy. Everyone's had some.'

Gabriel looks at me and I shake my head. 'I haven't had any.'

'You into it?'

'No.'

'Just have a go,' Aaron says.

'He doesn't have to.' Maddy scowls at Aaron.

'We're not staying here all day, are we?' I say.

'We've looked around already,' Fenton shrugs, 'seen everythin'.'

'Yeah, we're chillin',' Aaron says.

'Can't we go for a drink?' I say, aware that drink is something we all like. 'Anyone got ID?' It's always an issue, as only a couple of us are eighteen.

'I have,' James says.

'Cool.' I smile to myself, because there's no way James would get served without ID. He's tall, but skinny with spots.

'Where shall we go?' Maddy says.

'It has to be one of Amy's pubs.'

Maddy curls her lip. 'You what?'

'Amy Winehouse used to drink in The Hawley and The Castle. The Hawley's just back that way.' I point to the right.

'Sounds like a plan.' Maddy gets up, knowing everyone will follow.

Inside, the Hawley has some wood panelling, red walls and framed photos of famous musicians such as Joe Strummer from The Clash.

'It's one of them gastro pubs,' Aaron says. 'They hate young drinkers.'

But it's fine because James has ID and he gets the drinks in with the help of a whip-round and we find a table.

'Ren, they do an open mic night here,' Gabriel says.

'You should do it,' Carina says.

'I can't get here on a Monday. Susannah would go mental.'

'Tell her you're doing homework at mine,' Maddy says, 'they trust me.'

'Say you're the greatest undiscovered talent in Britain and you need to get out there and show people what you can do,' Gabriel says.

'I can't – not on a Monday.'

'Must be other open mic nights.' James does an internet search on his phone and comes up with different suggestions for every day of the week.

Maddy rolls her eyes at his geekiness.

'There's one tonight, The Slaughtered Lamb, Clerkenwell – starts at eight.'

'Slaughtered Lamb?' I don't like the sound of it.

'Website's cool.' James passes me his phone. The Slaughtered Lamb's home page has a quirky drawing of a wall-mounted trophy of a lamb's head.

'I've got no backing music.'

'Fenton can beatbox,' Aaron says.

Fenton's on his feet, snapback pushed back, doing *Back to Black*. People turn to look, Carina whoops and some girls clap along, while one stocky older bloke looks grumpy.

'Come on, Ren, join in, sing it,' Aaron says.

My heart races and I'm burning up.

A bearded member of staff comes over. 'Monday night's the night for that, mate. Come back then.'

I breathe out, like I've been saved. I want to simply sit and soak up the atmosphere, but there are too many of my mates here and the pub's too busy, like the everyday noise is blocking any chance of connecting with Amy. I look across the table. James is chatting up Maddy. She likes him, I think, but then she glances around checking on everyone else and I'm not so sure.

Gabe squeezes in next to me. 'You all right?' he says.

'Yeah, I just don't like people forcing me to sing.'

He shrugs. 'Even Amy Winehouse suffered with nerves.'

We stay there until our money runs out, which doesn't take long. Aaron and Fenton want to go into Soho, but it's so cold we decide to head back to Carina's. After the train, there's a bus that takes you to within metres of her front door and more importantly her parents are out. She has a free yard.

I text Susannah and tell her I'll be back at half eleven. She calls me straight back. 'Ren, you can't just text me and *tell* me what you're doing.'

I walk away to argue in private. 'Everyone's going.'

'Who's everyone?'

'There are loads of us.'

'Who exactly?'

'Maddy, Carina, Lily, Gabriel, Ross, Aaron, Fenton and James – satisfied?'

'You're being rude.'

'You're treating me like a little kid.'

'You're my responsibility. I must know where you are.'

'That's why I told you where I'm going and when I'll be back.'

'It's not for you to set a curfew.'

'No one else has to be back early. It's so unfair. You're making me look stupid.'

Eventually we compromise. I have to send Susannah Carina's address so that she can collect me. *Embarrassing.*

'You OK?' Gabriel comes over.

'I'm not having her turn up. I'll leave early – make my own way back.'

'I'll take you home – whenever you like.'

'Do you want to go to Carina's?'

He shrugs. 'I'm not bothered.'

'We could slope off, just us?'

He smiles. 'Let's do it.'

We head back to the tube station where there's a busker playing guitar and singing Dylan's *The Times They Are a-Changin'*. We stop to listen, and I don't know why but I guess it's because I've had a few drinks that I join in. And Maddy shoves me forward.

'Go, Ren,' Carina shouts, and Lily whoops.

The busker, a middle-aged guy in a flat cap, turns and smiles, and we attempt to duet. And I feel like it's working. I know the lyrics and I get through them right to the end and even manage to look up and meet people's eyes.

'What else d'you know?' the busker asks.

Maddy shouts, 'Anything by Amy Winehouse.'

And the busker strums the first few chords of *Rehab*, and I'm off like it's natural for me to sing in the street in front of a crowd of twenty or so people. I throw my head back and go for it, and at the end the busker goes straight into *Valerie* and people clap along.

People drop coins into a guitar case at the busker's feet. 'Thank you very much,' he says. 'God bless you, sir, very kind.'

'*You Know I'm No Good*,' I shout across to prompt the next choice of song. The crowd swells. There's clapping and cheers and more change is dropped into the guitar case.

At the end, I say, 'I've got to go. Thanks, it was really fun.'

'Wait.' The busker kneels down and tots up the takings. 'Here.' He passes me a handful of coins. 'You're good, any time you want to team up?'

'I don't live near here, sorry.'

'Shame,' he says, and shakes my hand.

'How much did you make?' Fenton asks.

'About a tenner.'

'You can buy some tinnies,' Aaron says.

I pass the cash to James and he goes into the nearest shop and buys some cans of "K" cider to share around.

We catch the train and as Gabe and me have our plan to slope off, we watch each other for the sign to get up and go.

Maddy picks up on it. 'What's the private joke?' she asks.

Gabe nods towards the door and we get up and wait for the train to stop.

Maddy raises an eyebrow. 'You're going?'

'What you doing?' Aaron asks.

'I've got to get back – family stuff,' I say.

Maddy frowns. 'You never said.'

'It just came up.'

'You as well, Gabe?' Aaron says.

'Sorry, mate.'

'That's well out,' Ross says, while Maddy gives me a look.

I wave as we jump off onto the platform, while Aaron and Ross make "wanker" signs through the window at Gabriel, but we just laugh and Gabe puts his arm around me.

'We can get the 371,' I say, as we leave the station.

'Let's walk. I hate buses. They're full of nutters.'

'We go on buses every day.'

'Exactly, that's how I know.'

'It's so cold.'

'I'll keep you warm.' He hugs me. 'Come on, let's run.' He pulls me along.

'You're too fast.'

We weave between people as we pass shops, restaurants and bars. 'Go down there.' I point towards Water Lane, which leads to the riverside. It's gone eight and the pubs are full. I peer into one of the windows. 'It looks so nice and warm in there.'

We walk under Richmond Bridge and Gabriel rushes ahead, climbs up and balances along a wall before jumping off the end.

'It's fun, try it.' He jumps onto one of the benches that are lined up in a long row. 'See how far I can get without touching the ground?'

'You're such a big kid.'

The benches are close enough to each other to jump from bench to bench. Gabe leaps between them until he reaches a larger gap. 'You can't do that,' I shout, but he jumps anyway and falls short.

'*Gabe*.' He's lying face down on the tarmac. I run over and kneel down beside him. '*Gabe, you OK?*'

He groans, rolls over and grabs me, pulling me down on top of him. 'You pig, you scared me.' I pull away, but he holds me firm and once he stops laughing, we kiss and continue like that even though the path's far too cold and damp to lie on.

'Will you still love me when you're famous?' he says, and I poke his ribs until he yelps and says, 'Let me up, babe,' and we both get up and walk hand in hand along the river and it's so beautiful in the lamplight with the moon reflected on the water.

'D'you ever write your own stuff?' he asks.

'Yeah, I try. It's no good though.'

We continue along the path and go through a gate into a field. 'There's cows here sometimes,' I say, 'must be like the only cows in London.'

'Nah, there's urban farms. I've been to one in Hounslow – only time I've ever seen cows.'

'No way. What about that trip to Devon?'

He smiles and holds me, and we kiss, and he then jogs ahead, pauses and does a backflip.

'Stop showing off.'

Again, he runs on ahead.

'*Wait!*'

Gabe stops at a fence and pulls himself up to look over the top. 'Let's explore – check out some gardens.'

'There might be cameras.'

'Put your hood up.'

'What if we set off an alarm?'

'It'll be fine. Come on, let's try here.' He shimmies up a wall, and looks over. 'Wow, look at that.'

'*Gabe.*'

'Don't be borin'.' He climbs over.

'*Gabriel.* What are you doing? Bloody hell, Gabe.' Oh, what the hell, I pull myself up the wall as best I can. I can't see much. There's a clump of trees. I hoist myself over and dangle down. Someone grabs my ankle. I gasp.

'Shush, I've got you, let go, jump down.'

I shut my eyes and do as he says. A few small twigs crack as I fall. My feet find a cushioned floor of rotting leaves. Gabriel catches me. 'I knew you could do it.' He strokes my face and a wave of warmth washes over me. He takes my hand and pushes branches aside until we can move forward, half crouched into the semi-open of the garden.

'Looks like the house in *American Horror Story*.' My heartbeat quickens. We're in the extensive grounds of a large old house. It's grand but run-down and creepy. 'Someone old must live here. They'll freak if they see us.'

'At least there won't be cameras, it's too overgrown for that, and they'll probably have bad eyesight and hearing. They may even be dead.'

'Don't say that. I want to go now.'

'Scaredy-cat.' Gabe pushes a strand of hair out of my eyes. 'I'll look after you. We'll just walk through, it'll be fine.' I believe him. He's there for me. He always will be, I know it. He loves me. I love him. It's for keeps. He kisses me and squeezes my hand, and we duck low and creep among the bushes, checking up at the windows from time to time. A light is switched on.

'In here, quick.' Gabriel moves between some trees. And I follow close behind. 'We need to find the perimeter.' He feels through the branches, as it's too dark to see and for a moment it feels like we could be in any ancient woodland, looking for a hollow way out. It reminds me of the enchanted but dangerous forests you get in fairy tales. My heart beats fast with both excitement and fear.

'Here we go.' He climbs a small tree.

'Can we get out there?'

'Almost.'

'What does that mean?'

'It's another garden.'

'*Gabriel*.' For some reason, I continue to disapprove when in reality I'm enjoying myself.

'It'll be OK.' He taps a lower branch. 'Climb up here.'

'No, wait.'

Gabriel goes over. And I follow, flipping over the wall into the next garden. My heart beats even faster. This place is smarter and therefore riskier. 'Oh no.'

'It's all right. Stay calm.' Gabriel beckons me to follow, as he crouches low and follows the garden's edge. Again, he slips between some bushes and finds a tree he can climb. It looks difficult, but he does it. 'We're all right. This is it.'

I struggle to hoist myself up and glance back. A security light flashes. *Shit.* I speed up and jump over the fence and fall, landing badly. I yelp in pain. My eyes are hot with tears. Gabriel rushes over. '*Ren*, you OK? What is it?'

'My ankle – it's killing.'

'Can you stand on it?'

I try. He has to hold me. 'I don't think I can walk.'

'How far to your house?'

'It's just up there.'

'Hold on to me. You'll have to hop on one leg.'

It takes ages to travel a short distance.

'What is it with you and trespassing?'

'It doesn't do any harm.'

'Apart from potentially scaring old ladies – and breaking my leg.'

'Is it cos I is black?' He does an Ali G voice.

'No, it's cos you're sneaking around on private property late at night. People are going to think the worst.'

'You telling me you didn't find it a buzz?'

'Seriously, I can live without it and now look at me.' We're at the gate to Ambrose House and I'm standing on one leg like a lame animal.

Gabe looks sheepish. 'That's not great.'

I key in the code and the gate opens.

'Ren, love you, but I've got to go.'

'Help me in at least.'

'I'm not into all that meetin' family stuff.'

'You've got to help.'

He kisses my cheek, and steps back. 'Sorry, I'm late.'

'*Gabe.*' I'm in too much pain to move. 'Help me to the door.'

He sighs and puts his arm around me and I can feel the strength and heat of his body as he helps me hop across the forecourt to the door.

'Slow down, what's your problem? You're rushing me. It hurts.'

He glances around like he's in trouble.

'Just ring the bell, will you? They'll help me in.'

'Hold onto that pot.' He guides me towards one of the large green glazed pots that sit either side of the front door, and dashes up the step, presses the buzzer and steps down. 'You'll be OK, yeah? Call me.' He kisses my cheek, turns and walks away.

'*Gabe.*'

Susannah opens the door. 'Ren? I thought I was collecting you.'

'Gabriel walked me back.' I nod in his direction, as I grip onto the large glazed pot.

'*Hello there,*' Susannah shouts.

Gabriel pauses. *Awkward.* And Susannah waves him back. 'Don't rush off.' He shuffles on the spot and Susannah dashes over, her hand outstretched. 'Nice to meet you, Gabriel,' she says. 'Come in.'

'I've got to get back.'

*Give up, Gabe, you don't stand a chance.* And so it is. After another few exchanges, he gives in and walks back, hands in his pockets. She's insistent like that. She can talk anyone around.

'Well, help me in then,' I say, keen to have him hold me once again.

Susannah frowns. 'What's the matter?'

'I've twisted my ankle.'

'How on earth did you do that?'

'Jumped off a wall near the river.'

'You did what – whereabouts?'

'Near that pub, you know, what's it called? The one near the bridge.'

'That's miles away. Have you hobbled all the way back like that? Heavens.'

I glance at Gabriel.

'It was a struggle,' he says.

'Took ages.'

'Well, let's get you in so we can have a proper look.'

Both Susannah and Gabriel help me into the Blue Room where I'm manoeuvred into a chair. Nicholas comes up from downstairs, surprised to see me back so early. He shakes Gabriel's hand (*cringe*) and stands behind Susannah as she inspects my ankle.

'Is it broken?' Alicia asks. 'You'll get a plaster. That's so cool. Can I draw on it?'

'I don't think it is,' Susannah says. 'The pain's reactionary rather than constant. You'll have to rest it for a few days.'

I groan. 'I've got plans.'

'You always have plans.'

'Are you at the same college, Gabriel?' Nicholas asks.

'Jeez,' I say, 'even in a medical emergency you obsess about education.'

'I'm just making conversation.'

'I'm at Cam's,' Gabriel says. 'It's near Bourne's.'

'What are you studying?'

'Maths, further maths, physics and chemistry.'

Nicholas nods his approval. 'What do you want to do after that?'

'I dunno.' He shrugs.

'No wonder he didn't want to come in,' I say.

Nicholas ignores that comment. 'You've applied for university?'

Gabe shakes his head. 'I don't want to be in debt.'

'How did you do in your GCSEs?' Susannah asks.

'He got eight A*s and two As,' I say.

'Impressive,' Susannah says. 'Your teachers must be encouraging you to carry on with your education?'

'Yeah, they've talked to my dad.'

'But you won't reconsider?'

'My dad wants me to go out to work – help out.'

That shut them up. What can they say to that? He's from a different world. Choice isn't something Gabriel believes in.

Susannah obviously goes away and thinks about it, because when she returns with a pack of frozen peas to rest on my ankle, she says. 'Have you thought of applying for a scholarship?'

He shuffles on the spot. 'No, not really.'

'How long do I have to stay like this?'

'You won't be going anywhere tomorrow, put it that way,' Susannah says.

'No way, what a fail, worst day of my life.'

Nicholas laughs. 'Your life must have been pretty good so far then.'

I look up to catch Gabriel's eye, but he's staring, open-mouthed, towards the French doors and the floodlit lake as if all this grandeur means something.

# TWENTY

Early morning, Susannah takes me to a walk-in minor injuries clinic – even though I can hardly "walk in".

'That's it, keep going.' Alicia leads the way, as I hobble along on my good foot.

It's a sprained ankle and I'm told to rest for a few days. Susannah confines me to the Hummingbird Suite, and makes me apply ice wrapped in a towel for twenty minutes every few hours while my right leg remains elevated on two plump pillows. I am given painkillers and all my meals arrive on a tray.

Monday lunchtime Susannah brings a hummus salad wrap and a smoothie. 'I could get used to this.'

'Don't get too comfortable,' Susannah says, 'I plan on getting you back to college by the end of the week even if I have to drop you myself.'

'I can't go to college like this. It's too painful.'

'The doctor said it's best to keep using the ankle if you can. You've got crutches. You'll cope.'

Gabriel skips football training after college and comes straight over. 'It's your *boyfriend*,' Alicia says, as she shows him in.

'Haven't you got Mandarin today?'

'My tutor's not here yet.'

'Do one.' I give her a look and Alicia pokes out her tongue as she leaves.

Gabriel kisses me and passes me chocolate. 'I got you this.'

'I love Lindt, thanks.'

'I feel really bad. It's all my fault.'

'Well, I may walk funny for the rest of my life, but don't worry about it.'

'I shouldn't have taken you all over the place like that.'

'To be honest, I enjoyed it. It's just I'm not very good at it.'

'Yeah?' He smiles. 'I was lookin' at this map and there's like this massive golf course near here. We could sneak in.'

'Why do you like trespassing so much?'

He shrugs. 'I don't see why any place should be shut to me, that's all.'

'What – like all property is theft?'

'People shouldn't be able to keep places to themselves. I don't get how some people can have so much?'

We both look around at the Hummingbird Suite with its golden wallpaper and fancy furniture and laugh.

'Your room's almost as big as my whole flat.'

'Seriously?'

'I'm exaggerating, but only just.'

'It *is* the Hummingbird Suite.'

'The wallpaper, yeah? Trini used to be called Land of the Hummingbird.'

'Trini?'

'Trinidad – where my dad's from. There's a word that means Land of the Hummingbird.'

'I'll Google it.' I look it up on my phone. '"The original name for the island in the Arawaks' language was '*Iere*', which meant Land of the Hummingbird." I'd love to see a real hummingbird.'

'We'll go there one day.'

I love that he says that. It makes it sound like we'll always be together. 'That would be awesome,' I say. 'Have you been?'

'No, never.' He goes to the wall behind me to get a closer look at the wallpaper. 'This is hand-painted, I reckon.'

'Amazing, isn't it? I can stare at it for ages.'

He moves behind me and massages my neck, making me tingle. 'Got you where I want you at last. No escape.' He kisses the top of my spine. 'Your tattoo – that's ultramarine blue?'

'Is it?' I wonder if I should know that. Gabe's always coming out with facts that I feel I should know but don't.

'It used to be the most expensive colour – made from lapis lazuli. D'you know what ultramarine means?'

'Let me guess, ultra-blue, super blue?'

'It means "beyond the sea" – it was imported from Asia.'

'Beyond the sea – I like that.' He makes me think my tattoo is special, precious and exotic.

'Artists only used it on really special things like Jesus's or Mary's clothes.'

'You know what my dad was saying about uni? Perhaps he's right. Someone as bright as you should go.'

'I thought you weren't bothered about all that?'

'I've been thinking I probably do need a backup, especially as I get so nervous performing.'

'Are you feelin' all right?'

'No, I can't walk.'

'I gotta try your crutches.' He picks up the sticks and swings his lean, fit body across the room and into the en suite. 'Just need a piss.'

'Charming.'

He goes in, leaving the door slightly ajar, and soon returns on crutches.

'I hope you washed your hands.'

''Course I did.' He puts the crutches down and kisses me.

There's a knock at the door.

It's Maddy. She looks from me to Gabe and back again. 'Have I interrupted something?'

'No,' I say, feeling myself redden.

'How's the ankle?' she asks.

'Sore. How was college?'

'Dull.'

'Well, it would be without me.'

'I mean dull as usual. How long are you going to be like that?'

'Dunno. Susannah's allowing me two or three days off and then I've got to go in on crutches.'

'What, on the bus?'

'No, she'll drop me off.'

'I reckon you did it deliberately to avoid that open mic night in Camden.'

'I've been thinking about that. I'm going to try a few nights around here before I go to Camden – less pressure.'

'Are there any around here?' Gabriel asks.

'Yeah, there's a few. They sound small and I think that might make it worse. You know, too claustrophobic, like I'll be really closely scrutinised.'

'People will just carry on drinkin' and chattin',' Gabriel says. 'You'll be background music.'

'Thanks.'

'Everyone has to start somewhere,' Maddy says. 'But, saying that, you have had over 45,000 views of that first video and the second's up to 3,000 now.'

Gabe smiles. 'You have been watchin' yourself a lot.'

'Very funny.'

'When are these open mic nights?' Maddy asks.

'There's two on Mondays and one on Wednesday.'

'You can go tonight,' Gabriel says.

'*Hello*, have you not noticed my ankle?'

'Don't sing with your ankle, do you?'

'There's no way Susannah will let me out tonight.'

'Wednesday she might,' Maddy says. 'You could be up and about by then.'

'You don't have to tell her what you're doin',' Gabriel says.

'I suppose you think I should climb out the window and walk through everyone's gardens.'

'What? I don't get that.' Maddy narrows her eyes. 'Was this caused by Parkour or free running or whatever it's called?' She looks at Gabriel, her chin tilted upwards. 'Is it your fault Ren's like this?'

'It's not his fault, though I guess I shouldn't have followed.'

'You *were* doing that running thing.'

'Are you crazy? D'you really think I'd do all that jumping between buildings? No way.'

'Anyway, back to the open mic sessions,' Gabriel says. 'Why don't you aim for next week? You'll be walkin' by then.'

'I'll probably be on crutches.'

'It could work in your favour. People aren't going to laugh at a cripple.'

I throw a cushion at him. 'Thanks a lot.'

We hang out for another half an hour or so, when Gabe says he has to get back as he has "work to do".

'I'll come with you,' Maddy says. 'I hate waiting at bus stops on my own.'

I find this weird as I thought she'd want to stay and catch up. 'You only just got here.'

'Got loads to do. I'm really behind on my coursework.'

They let themselves out, Gabe stepping back to let Maddy go first.

Alone, it feels too quiet so I scroll through the music on my phone hoping noise will fill the emptiness.

# TWENTY-ONE

Mum and Jay were due up at the weekend to go Christmas shopping, but due to my sprained ankle they've postponed. Mum suggested we make it the week after, but it's Aaron's party on the Saturday so we've rearranged for three weeks' time.

So, I've got Aaron's party the week after next, Mum and Jay up the week after that and then there's only a few more weeks at college before the Christmas break. It's going to be the best Christmas ever. It's all arranged: four days in Devon at Mum's, then back to London where I'll catch a plane to Saint Lucia with Nicholas, Susannah and Alicia. Saint Lucia, as in the Caribbean – a holiday with proper sunshine, amazing beaches, warm sea and cocktails.

'You're a lucky girl,' Mum says over the phone.

I lie back on my bed, staring at the ornate cornicing in the Hummingbird Suite. 'I hope my ankle's all right by then.'

'Don't go jumping off any more walls. Whose idea was it anyway? I bet it was that new boyfriend of yours?'

'It wasn't his fault.'

'I bet you were drunk. How many times have I told you about the risks of binge-drinking?'

'I only had two drinks, chill out, and that was hours before anyhow. We'd been up in Camden. I got a new tattoo.'

'You'd better be winding me up? You know what I said when you had the last one done.'

'You liked it in the end. You said it was pretty … for a tattoo.'

'You promised me you wouldn't get any more.'

'Chill, I haven't really, they wouldn't do it.'

'Good, you're perfect as you are.'

'Everyone's mum says that.'

'Yeah, well, I don't always say it.'

'That's nice.' We're mates really. For years I've given her a hard time, but we get on now, especially as we're no longer in each other's faces. Mum's all right. 'I miss you,' I say.

'I miss you too, I really do. You have no idea. And you've made me cry now, and I've just done my make-up for work.' I think of Bella's Café in Exeter where Mum spends her days serving pensioners, students and tourists.

'Don't go – skive off.'

'I can't do that.'

'That cow Yvonne's always calling in sick.'

'Doesn't mean I should do the same.'

'I wish you lived in London. It would be so much better if you were here. Can't you move back?'

'London's not for me. My life's down here now.'

'You didn't really give it a chance.'

Nine months she lived in London and that was years ago, before I was born, although apparently I was there for part of it – in her belly that is. She was pregnant and that's why she left. It wasn't working between her and Nicholas and she needed to be near her mum and dad, and that meant Devon.

What is it with Mum and Nicholas? Why didn't it work? I have asked but the answer is never enough. I try again. 'I asked Nicholas what happened between you two, but he said he'd have to speak with you first.'

'Did he now?'

'I've got a right to know.'

'It's water under the bridge. Mind you, I'm not going to discuss it over the phone. We'll talk when I see you. Have you sorted out where we're going? We need somewhere to eat that's not too expensive.'

It's weeks away and I have other things to think about.

The ankle's healing well. I need the crutches but I'm up and about. Susannah drops me and picks me up for a couple of days and then I tell her to stop. I can cope, though I'll have to take a backpack rather than my usual bag.

It's good that I do because it means she stops fussing and lets me go out.

Gabe calls around Monday evening but it turns out he can't take me to the open mic night. 'I've got to get back and help my dad.'

'Why, what have you got to do?'

'I've got to get a few bits and cook.'

'Why can't he do all that?'

'He's workin' late.'

'I could help? How about I help cook, then I could meet your dad at the same time.'

Gabe looks askance as he steps back.

'I'd like to meet your dad.'

'OK…' he says in a long, drawn-out way that makes me think it's not OK.

'It's weird I've not been to your place or met your dad.'

He shrugs. 'We're always over this way. It takes ages to get to mine, and you can hardly move as it is.'

'I don't even know your address,' I say, even though this hadn't bothered me until Maddy brought it up, saying it was suspicious that he hadn't taken me there and that I'd be stupid not to ask why.

Gabe shrugs. 'There's no secret.'

'What is it then? Where do you live?'

'You know where I live.'

'Only vaguely – I don't know the address.'

He frowns. 'I'll write it down for you if you like.'

'Yeah, do.'

'What's the big deal?'

'I don't know, you tell me?'

He paces the room. 'It's like you don't trust me.'

'What if I wanted to send you something?'

'Like what?'

'I dunno, a birthday present?'

He sucks his teeth. 'You'd give it me in person.'

'I might want to order something online. Look, there's paper and a pen on the desk, you can write it there.'

He scrawls the address and drops the pen.

'Are you ashamed of me, is that it? I mean there's got to be something I don't know?'

He frowns. 'Why are you bein' like this? You don't trust me?'

'It's like I don't know enough about you. I don't get why you haven't invited me over, unless you've got something to hide?'

He groans. 'You're causin' an argument for no reason. I'm out of here.'

'You said you'd take me to the open mic night?'

'I can't, I told you: I've got to cook. I'd say another night, but it doesn't seem like fun any more.'

'Is that it then? You bail on me as soon as I want to know a little bit more?'

'You're doin' my head in.'

'My friends think you must be hiding something.'

'Yeah, is that what you think?'

I don't answer.

'Fine, have it your way. See you around.'

He walks out. No kiss, no backward glance. And part of me wishes I'd never asked. I mean it wasn't really bothering me until Maddy brought it up. She made me question what I thought and that made me question Gabe and now he thinks that I think less of him than I do.

# TWENTY-TWO

The Racing Page is a small local pub that holds a weekly open mic night in a function room upstairs. I'm not in the mood after arguing with Gabe and it's a bit of a struggle, what with the crutches, but I manage to get up the stairs and thankfully no one asks my age because it would be so humiliating to have to turn around and immediately struggle back down again – not only a cripple, but an underage one as well.

The room's half-full and most of the people are turned towards a long-haired man in his twenties who's playing an acoustic guitar and singing Leonard Cohen's *Hallelujah*, though I presume he thinks it's more the Jeff Buckley version.

We approach the bar, but are intercepted by a skinny woman with dark curly hair. She's holding a clipboard. 'Are you ladies looking to perform tonight?'

Maddy nudges me. 'She is.'

'Great, I'll put you down.' The woman looks up, her pen poised above her clipboard. 'What's your name?'

I want to back out. It's an immediate crisis of confidence. 'Sorry, I'm just going to listen tonight, it's too awkward.' I hold up one of my crutches.

'Don't worry about that. You've not got far to go, see. What's your name? I'll put you down. We've a few slots free.'

'No, sorry, I'm just here to watch this time. Next week.' I turn away so that she can't pitch me again.

'What's the matter?' Maddy says. 'You've got to take every

opportunity. How else are you going to get used to performing? You've got over 50,000 hits on your videos now. You need to get out there and get noticed, especially if I'm going to be your manager.'

'Manager?' I smile. 'You're just nagging me. You're as bad as Susannah. What is it with everyone tonight?'

A large woman of about thirty is next. She's pretty with straight brown hair. It's difficult to hear her and someone has to adjust the microphone.

She sings *Summertime* in a controlled and powerful voice. 'She's good,' I say, my voice breaking with emotion.

'No better than you.' Maddy looks into my eyes. I can tell that she's aware I'm emotional but she ignores it. 'You need to get up there,' she says.

'I don't want to, not tonight, OK. I just want to listen and watch, see what it's like. I'll come back next week.'

Maddy curls her lip. 'We'll see.'

'I'll practise and then come back. I want to get it right. Anyway, it's not like I have to rush. I'm not even eighteen.'

The lady with the clipboard takes the mike. 'We're going to take a short break now,' she says. 'Back in ten.'

'See, they haven't got enough acts tonight,' Maddy says.

'Oh, for God's sake.' I swing across the bar on my crutches. 'Are there any slots left?' I ask the lady with the clipboard.

She looks at me with eyes as hard as buttons. 'It's all yours if you go now.'

I have no backing track and I know it'll be bad. Eyes closed, I take the mike and sing *Our Day Will Come* – a song of love and optimism that Amy covered. I look at no one, and think only of Gabe and the rift that has opened so unexpectedly between us. Please, let it be OK, I think and tears well in my eyes.

Clipboard-woman comes up to me afterwards. 'How old are you?'

'I'm…' I almost give it away. 'I'm eighteen.'

She nods. 'Come back next week. I've got a friend coming – he's in A&R.'

'A&R?' I don't know what she means.

'He's a talent scout for a new indie label.'

Maddy looks smug, her nose and chin tilted upwards. 'I told you it would be worth it.'

'Whatever.' I know I should be glad and I am, but there's only one person I want to tell and he's not taking my calls.

I text him anyway: 'Just did open mic x'.

# TWENTY-THREE

I play certain songs on repeat: *Back To Black* and *Love Is A Losing Game*, along with The Shangri-Las' *I Can Never Go Home Anymore*, which was the song Amy listened to whenever she split with Blake.

Gabriel's gone from my life. I've not seen him on the bus, at Chicken Shack or after college, and there are only so many messages you can send without receiving a reply.

Back home in my room, I sit on the floor and write lyrics in a notebook, which I mostly scribble out. I have pages of fragments, song ideas and the odd chorus that needs a few verses to make it work. At the mirror, I sing *Back To Black* before going to bed, headphones on, to listen to Amy.

'You look terrible.' I didn't even hear Alicia come in.

'Thanks for that. Can you go now?'

'Why are you crying?'

'I'm not.' I wipe smeared mascara from my face. 'Can you get out, please?'

*How can it be normal to break up and not know why? Have we broken up?* I check Gabe's Facebook page. He's not posted anything and it still says he's "in a relationship" with me.

I find Susannah in the snug and tell her I don't feel well.

'What's the matter?'

'I've got a stomach ache. I feel sick.'

Her eyes look kind, but she says, 'I suggest you get a good night's sleep and sort yourself out. I don't believe in days off.'

Again Gabriel's not on the bus. I check my phone a million

times. *Where are you, Gabe? What's going on?*

'He's changed and I don't know why,' I tell Maddy, as we sit in the common room before lunch.

'Something must have happened.' She waits for an explanation. 'I take it you had a fight?'

'It doesn't make sense,' I say. 'It's like he doesn't want to invite me back and introduce me to his dad for some reason.'

'I told you he's hiding something. He should introduce you.' Maddy shakes her head. 'There's more to it.'

'Do you think?'

'He's seeing someone else. You were right to ask him.'

My stomach twists at the thought. 'He's not like that.'

'But you don't know, do you?'

'I guess not.'

'Most guys mess around, given the chance. Why else would he not take you back? He must be seeing someone near where he lives or he'd invite you back.'

'Maybe you're right.' I feel sick inside.

'Tell him where to go.'

'I would if he was talking to me.'

'Text him.'

'I don't think he's even reading my messages.'

'You're joking? Who does he think he is? His loss. Sod him.' Her expression softens. 'We need to get you out and about so you can forget about it and move on. Come over to mine tonight. I've got a free yard.'

'You've got James coming over?'

'He can come any time. I'll ditch him for you.' She smiles, her eyes intense. 'Girlfriends come first, you know that.'

'OK.' I'm grateful that like a real friend she's there for me.

Late out of college, I rush to catch up with Maddy. I can see her ahead. She's at the bus stop. She's talking to Gabe. My insides twist.

*Can I turn around, go another way, or even better disappear?* I fear it's too late. There are too many people around. I watch as Gabe says something and Maddy laughs. I don't want to catch up. I hang back and watch. Maddy's animated, like she's trying to entertain and Gabe does smile, look down and laugh, and that annoys me. My heart races as I draw nearer. *I can't catch up. What would I say?* Convinced they haven't noticed me, I duck into a newsagent's where I study a magazine without taking in a single word.

Mr and Mrs Costa are working late, "stocktaking", Maddy says when I arrive at her place later on. The fridge is empty, so we order pizza, dough balls and ice cream and go on the computer: Facebook, Tumblr and WhatsApp, checking out any guy we can think of – mainly to take the piss.

'Butters,' I say, at the sight of Carl Worthington.

'What about David Hillier?'

'No way, look at that hair.'

I'm all right like that, messing about, even though deep down Gabe's there, lurking in the dark recesses of my mind, twisting my insides, causing me pain. But I don't tell Maddy any of that. I tell her I'm OK, over him in fact, and that yes, I will go to Chicken Shack, why shouldn't I? He doesn't own it.

Chicken Shack, the next day, and Carina asks if I'm "OK with this?"

'Yeah, course, it's not his place.' But my stomach churns and I order only fries and a drink and pick at the food, wishing I was elsewhere. The worst happens. Aaron pushes the door, shrieks, looks back and makes a gesture at his throat as if Gabriel's in trouble.

I want to run out, but I force myself to remain.

Gabriel stares ahead, only glancing briefly in my direction. *What is it? What have I done?* As soon as the lads are at the counter, I'm out the door and breathing again, tears in my eyes as I walk back to college.

'He is such a dumb arse,' Carina says.

Maddy glances back through Chicken Shack's window. 'Let's go out tonight – take your mind off it? We could see a film or something?'

Carina makes a face. 'I can't tonight.'

Maddy pretends to yawn. 'Don't tell me, you're seeing Idris?' She arches an eyebrow, tuts and shakes her head.

Back home I eat organic, corn-fed, free-range chicken with Susannah and Alicia and then head out, and I'm nearly at Maddy's when my phone pings with a text from Gabriel – one word: 'Sorry'.

I text back: '?'

Gabriel: 'I can explain'

Me: 'Yeah?'

Gabriel: 'Come over?'

Me: 'Why?'

Gabriel: 'We can talk'

Me: 'Not bothered'

Gabriel: 'Don't be like that'

Me: 'Like what?'

Gabriel: 'Pissed with me'

Me: 'Why not?'

Gabriel: 'Let me explain'

Me: 'Won't help'

Gabriel: 'Please?'

Me: 'Can't'

Gabriel: 'Why not?'

Me: 'Going out'

Gabriel: 'Where?'

I glance up briefly from my phone and lean against a wall.

Me: 'With a friend'

Gabriel: 'Who?'

Me: 'Does it matter?'

Gabriel: 'What's the problem?'

Me: 'You'

Gabriel: 'Don't be like that'

Me: 'Are you serious?'

Gabriel: 'It's not what you think'

Me: 'You disappeared'

Gabriel: 'It's not how it looks'

Me: 'Yeah?'

Gabriel: 'When can I see you?'

Me: 'Don't know'

Gabriel: 'Come on?'

Me: 'Busy'

Gabriel: 'Tomorrow?'

Me: 'Got plans'

Gabriel: 'What?'

Me: 'Washing my hair'

Gabriel: 'You're killing me'

Me: 'Can you blame me?'

Gabriel: 'Please let me explain?'

Me: 'Go ahead'

Gabriel: 'I have to see you'

Me: 'Invite me round'

Gabriel: 'OK'

Me: 'OK?'

Gabriel: 'You know where I live'

Me: 'Yeah'

Gabriel: 'Come round after college'

Me: 'K'

Gabriel: 'Meet me outside Bourne's'

Me: 'Make it Chicken Shack'

# TWENTY-FOUR

I don't bother telling Maddy about the texts from Gabe or plans to meet. What if he doesn't show up? Telling Maddy or anyone else would make it even worse.

Mr and Mrs Costa are out again, so we help ourselves to tumblers of ouzo mixed with lemonade, and a giant bag of nachos.

'There's nothing worth seeing,' I say, as I check the cinema listings.

'Let's stay in and download *Texas Chainsaw Massacre.*'

It's not really my thing but I go along with it anyway.

Susannah calls halfway through. 'Be back by eight.'

I roll my eyes and say, 'You treat me like I'm five.'

'It's dark already. You're lucky I'm letting you stay out that late.'

I end the call. 'She does my head in.' Sometimes I think life was easier back in Devon. Mum gives me far more freedom.

We watch the film. 'I didn't really like that,' I say, as the credits roll. 'And now I've got to get home on my own.' I make a face like I'm scared.

'You choose tomorrow's film – my parents are out again.'

'I can't do tomorrow.'

'How come?'

I feel myself redden. 'I've got to catch up on my artwork.'

'Forget that – you've got the weekend.'

'Miss Floyd's on at me. I've got to do it.'

'You can come for a bit?'

'Another night,' I say, thinking of Gabe.

The following day I stay late at college, making out I need to catch up in the art room. Maddy and Carina come looking for me.

'That's where you're hiding,' Maddy says, looking over my work.

'We're going for waffles,' Carina says, 'you want to come?'

'I've got to finish off. I'm really behind.' I gesture towards the textured A1 drawing in front of me. 'I'll be ages.'

'How long?' Carina asks.

The drawing's about ninety per cent complete, but I assume they won't realise. 'I've got to annotate everything ready to give in tomorrow.'

Maddy curls her lip. 'Doesn't sound like you. Can't you rush it?'

Carina nods. 'Since when have you cared so much?'

I take a deep breath in an attempt to quash my rising panic that they're making me late and that Gabe might not wait. 'No, really, I need to carry on. Don't wait for me.'

'We'll piss off then, leave the neek to it,' Maddy says. 'You better be out Saturday though – Aaron's party. You promised you'd go to that.'

'There's no way I'd miss that,' I say, knowing I owe Maddy that.

'Catch you later.' Carina makes an "L" for loser sign by her forehead as they go out the door.

Immediately, I scrabble my stuff together, chucking pencils and pens into my pencil case, and sliding my artwork into my folder.

'Careful with that,' Miss Floyd says. 'I don't want you handing in shoddy goods.'

Outside, there's drizzly rain. I put up my umbrella to protect my art folder and then struggle to hold everything and run. But I'm catching up with Maddy and Carina and have to slow down. My heart thumps as I hang back. I take a right and can finally see the turquoise sign with the words "Chicken" and "Shack" separated by a red love heart.

*Where is he?* I search the street for Gabriel, and check my watch. *Twelve minutes late – has he gone?* I walk past the window and try to peer in as if it's a casual glance. It's pretty busy. I can't see him. I continue walking and searching, looking all around.

There he is. He's leaning against a shop doorway, checking his phone. I slow down and watch him concentrating as he texts. He's as beautiful as ever and my heart beats fast, but it's with an added sense of danger. This boy can hurt me and has done.

He senses me there watching him, and looks up and smiles. I don't move, and he comes to me, an intense but warm look on his face. 'Ren,' he says, but it's awkward, and as he goes to hug me I step back. 'Oh, OK,' he says, 'fair enough.' He offers me his hand, but I shake my head.

'Shall we go in Chicken Shack?'

Again, I shake my head. 'Let's walk.'

'It's been the worst week,' he says, and I tighten my grip on the handle of my art folder, annoyed that he can say this when the week's been way worse for me as I've not known what it's all about.

'You ignored my texts,' I say.

'No.' He shakes his head. He's adamant and it's convincing.

'I kept texting. You didn't answer.'

'My phone was playin' up,' he says.

'And your computer?'

He makes a face like he knows he was wrong.

'I assumed it was over.'

'Never think that.' He grabs my hand but I pull it away.

'You changed,' I say, 'I don't get why.'

He shakes his head. 'It's stupid – I'm stupid.'

'There's someone else?'

It's like I've pushed him back and said something I shouldn't have. 'I'm not like that,' he says.

'What then, because I don't get it – what have I done wrong?'

We stop in the middle of the street, a little away from a cluster of benches where people could overhear. It's no longer raining but the sky remains grey and people are rushing past. Gabriel looks away and then back. 'It's me. I'm an idiot.'

'You're seeing someone else?'

He shakes his head firmly. 'I'd never do that – not to you, not to anyone. That's too like my mum. That's insulting.'

'Explain it then. What's going on?'

He's silent like he's wrestling with something big in his head.

'Just tell me – what's the problem?'

He looks away for a moment, turns back and says, 'Where I live – the estate – it's a dump.'

'I'm sure it's not that bad, but even if it is, why would that be relevant?'

'It's a shithole.' He looks down at his shoes.

I shrug. 'I don't care where you live.'

'You're so rich.'

'I'm not.'

'You live in a mansion.'

'My dad's got money, I haven't.'

'Your dad's a multimillionaire.'

'It's not like I'm rich.'

'It's what you're used to – you'll think less of me.'

'You're forgetting my mum's normal-sized house in Devon. I was there until recently. I've never cared where you live or what your house is like.'

'I'm embarrassed about where I live, even though I know I shouldn't be, which makes me feel crap in itself because I know my dad's doin' his best, but then again he annoys me anyway because he's so judgemental.' He gently touches my shoulder to guide me out of the way as a large group barge past.

'What d'you mean your dad's judgemental?'

'I don't like introducin' people. He can be really negative.'

'The thing is, if you don't introduce me it's like I'm not

important to you.' I blink and try to hold it together.

'Ren, you're the best thing that's happened to me.' He takes both my hands but I pull away. 'I mean it. I don't want to lose you.' Again, he reaches out to hold me and this time I let him. 'You're everything.' Normally I'd laugh at such a comment, like it's cheesy, but he looks at me with the most loving, beautiful look ever and I know it's for real. 'I mean it,' he says.

I know, I think, and we kiss and it's the best kiss, the sort of kiss that takes you out of yourself. To anyone else it might look like two teenagers making out in the middle of a damp pedestrianized shopping precinct, but to me it's like we're outside time and space in the best possible place where this true and absolute emotion permanently marks our memories – Ren and Gabe forever.

It's my greatest, happiest moment, and if I only have this, already I have more than some people ever know.

Everything stops, the world falls away, nothing else matters. It was all a misunderstanding. We're back together. We kiss again, and then pull back and look at one another like we've never really looked before.

'Your eyes are blue-grey,' he says, 'like English sky.'

'What do you mean – overcast, dull?'

'Kind of delicate – nothing obvious, unpredictable even – you're beautiful.' He holds my face in his hands and looks so lovingly, while I study his light hazel eyes with their little dark flecks and darker rim.

'Your eyes are tortoiseshell,' I say.

'At least you didn't say turtle.'

'I love turtles.'

He strokes my face and my heart is flying, weightless, not a care in the world. 'Time to go back to mine?' He takes my hand and leads me to the bus stop, where we catch the H22 and sit at the back.

The bus stops at the station, where Gabe normally swaps to or from my bus, and then travels onwards to parts of town I've never been. At first it's suburban with mock-Tudor semis that give way to small boxy houses, broken up by an occasional row of shops. The sky darkens, and the bus stops become busier: a tattooed woman with a pram, a man with shopping and two old ladies chatting. I offer them our seats.

'Very kind of you, my love.'

I stare out at the buildings: small supermarkets with vegetables outside like market stalls, a Lebanese café and a pound shop.

Gabriel rings the bell, and we disembark by a Polish deli. He takes my hand as we turn right towards a series of concrete tower blocks.

I wrap my coat tighter, as we head into the wind.

A low wall marks the boundary of the Crane Hill Estate, and a plain tarmac path cuts through an area of neat grass towards the first grey block.

Two young kids on BMXs cut in front of us as we approach Hogarth House.

'I also have to key in a code.' Gabriel inputs numbers into a metal keypad. Someone's leaving – a lady with grey bobbed hair. She smiles at Gabriel and holds the door open for him.

'Thanks, Caroline,' he says, and in turn holds the door open for me to follow him into a brown tiled reception area where there are two metal doors to the left. 'Can't trust the lift,' he says, 'it's always breakin' down.'

'How far up are you?'

'It's five floors. Can you cope with your ankle?'

I nod. 'Sure, though I'll take a while.' And Gabe opens the door to the stairwell, which is painted parsley green. The lighting's too bright, making it seem harsh, hollow and hostile.

'How many floors are there?'

'Twenty-six.'

'Must be an awesome view up there.'

Gabe checks around and whispers, 'Jamil's on the twentieth. You can see for miles up there – right into central London.'

'Why are you whispering?'

'I don't talk to Jamil.'

'How come?'

Gabe sucks his teeth. 'He's with a different crowd.'

'What, like a gang?'

He looks away, creases between his brows. 'I avoid all that.' He gets out his key and opens a brown door. 'After you.'

The hallway's a lemon box room, leading to a bright yellow living area.

'Someone likes yellow.'

'It's my dad,' Gabe says, 'he's longin' for sunshine.'

There's a black leather sofa, a pine coffee table with a Bible on it, a TV and a framed poster of a tropical beach. 'Is that Trinidad?'

Gabe nods, and shouts, 'Dad?' There's a clanking sound before a tall man, aged anywhere between thirty-five and fifty fills the kitchen doorway.

He's darker than Gabe, and his hair is greying at the sides. Barefoot, in jeans and a denim shirt, with a thick gold chain, he's held onto his looks better than most middle-aged men. He nods briefly at me, turns to Gabe and says, 'Did you get milk?'

Gabriel retrieves a carton from his rucksack. 'This is my friend, Ren,' he says. 'This is my dad, Michael.'

'Nice to meet you,' I say, my hand ready to shake his but unsure whether he'll offer. He doesn't and I discreetly lower my hand, hoping no one notices. 'It's a great view you have.' We all look towards the large window and its view of the A316, flats, houses, and beyond.

'If you like concrete,' he says.

I nod towards the poster. 'Trinidad looks beautiful.'

He narrows his eyes. 'It is beautiful, but it's lost to me.'

'That's cheerful, Dad. Come on, I'll show you my room.' Gabe gestures for me to follow, and I smile at Mr Walker to let him know that I'd be happy to stay and chat to him, but his brow lowers.

He disapproves. Perhaps I shouldn't go to Gabe's room, but what harm can it do? It's only a room. I follow Gabe because I want to be with him and I also want to see his place and know what it's like.

Gabe's room is small with a single bed, a desk and a neat row of trainers in one corner and a poster of Bob Marley on the wall above the bed.

'Your dad doesn't like me.'

Gabe lies back on the burgundy duvet, while I perch at the bed's edge. 'It'll be cos you're happy to go to my room. Dirty mind, innit.'

My mood plummets, unhappy that his dad thinks the worst of me when all I feel for Gabe is love.

'Ignore him,' Gabe says, as he sits up and kisses my neck.

'He might come in.' I shift away. 'Where's your loo?'

'Next door.' He points.

The bathroom's not had the sunshine yellow treatment. It's brown with a smoked glass mirror that makes everything look like it's from ancient history – maybe as far back as the Seventies.

'What's with the Bob Marley poster?' I ask, as I re-enter Gabe's room. 'I didn't know you were a fan.'

'One love.'

'Don't worry about a thing…'

'Bob knew what he was talking about.'

'I don't think your dad likes me.'

'He's like that with everyone. Doesn't want me messin' around. It's deep, but he thinks it best I don't date white girls because it didn't work out for him.'

'That's racist.'

He nods. 'Yep.'

'You don't care?'

'I'm seein' you, aren't I?'

'You almost finished it.'

'You'll finish it now you've seen where I live and met my dad.'

'He's not you.'

In the light from the lamp on Gabe's desk, his expression appears soft and kind, with a look in his eye that has to be true love.

My phone goes. It's Susannah. 'Ren, where are you?'

'I'm at Gabe's.' I roll my eyes and Gabe smiles and lies back on the bed.

'I thought that was over.'

'What gave you that idea?'

'Alicia said you were upset.'

'She had no right to say that.'

'Where does Gabriel live?'

'Um – Gabe, where are we again?'

'Hounslow,' he says loud enough for Susannah to hear.

'You need to come home,' she says, her voice lower.

'Why?'

'It's late.'

'No, it's not.'

'I don't want you there.'

'What – why?'

'It's not a good area.'

'I'm with Gabe, it's fine.'

'Ren, it's already dark. What were you thinking? Where does he live? Are you on an estate?'

'Yeah, but then posh people live on estates.'

'Ren, this is no laughing matter. Youths have been killed there.'

'You're making that up and who the hell says "youths"?'

'There have been stabbings – recently. I want you home now. Get Gabriel to walk you to the bus stop and put you on the correct bus.'

'I've only just got here.'

'It's not for discussion. Leave now, otherwise I'm phoning Nicholas and your mother.'

'But, it's not even six o'clock.'

'I don't care. I want you out of there.'

'Oh, for God's sake.'

'*Now*, I mean it.'

I end the call. 'Jeez, that woman is nuts.'

Gabe shrugs. 'I didn't even get to jump your bones.'

I lean over, and he pulls me down and again it's like the whole world and all that's good, bad and indifferent melts away.

# TWENTY-FIVE

I'm grounded. How pointless is that. I wish Alicia were older, and had already trained Susannah in the art of parenting a teenager because right now she's clueless. So what I didn't tell her I was going to Gabe's and yeah, OK, he lives on an estate and it's not the greatest area, but it's not as if anything bad happened. If Susannah met Gabe's dad I swear they'd get on because he's a super-strict, Jesus-loving control freak and, OK, Susannah's not religious, unless you count how she worships superfoods and anything organic, hand-reared, free-range, line-caught, gluten-free or whatever, but she's definitely a control freak.

There's no point in grounding me. It doesn't do any good. Mum used to do it in Year Eight and it didn't do anything. She stopped in the end, just as she gave up on the naughty step all those years before. Strictness is not her thing. She's one of those single mums who are also your best friend, so instead we fight like mates and that leads to other complications.

Susannah says that after college I must go straight home. No hanging in cafés, parks or council estates in Hounslow or anywhere else. She fears for my safety and indeed my very life.

'There have been killings,' she said, her face all red the evening I got back from Gabe's (having stayed another forty minutes after she called). 'There are gangs and they're stabbing each other. I looked it up. They're dealing drugs. It's there in the local paper and on the Internet.'

She needs to get a grip. It's not all *Top Boy* and gangsters in the hood. Gabe isn't involved in any of that. The only gang he knows includes Aaron, Fenton, James and Ross and they're the biggest pussies, in the nicest way.

Yeah, OK, he knows Jamil, or he used to, and I dare say he knows a lot of other kids on the estate that have gone in the wrong direction, but he avoids them. He's head down, earning the grades to get out and work and help his dad.

I tell Susannah all of this, every day after college when I'm back super-early, trapped in that luxury prison with its joyless freaky food.

I've taken to swimming in an attempt to work off my anger and frustration, swearing at Susannah with every stroke. My ankle has strengthened and my arms are developing contours I didn't know possible while my stomach's tightened and flattened. I'm going to look dank at Aaron's party, or at least I will if Susannah lets me go. She's grounded me for a week. 'Perhaps you'll learn to keep us informed of your whereabouts,' she said, her cheeks sucked in and it was like I could tell the shape of her skull beneath her skin. You should eat some sugar and fat, I thought. I mean the rest of England may be obese but Susannah is off the scale the other way.

'You can't ground me, you're not my mum.' This was probably the worst, most inflammatory thing I could have said. Alicia sucked in air and awaited the explosion and even I thought, shit, what have I said?

'You're not my daughter but I am married to your father and while you live in my house you abide by my rules. You're my responsibility. London's not like Devon. It is far more dangerous. Young people are stabbed and killed on a regular basis and I will not let you throw your life away by hanging out in the wrong places. This boy Gabriel, how do you know he's not involved in drugs and gangs? Well?'

'He's not like that. You're so judgemental. He works harder than me. He's never been in trouble.'

'How did you really hurt your ankle? Were you running from someone or did he push you?'

'You're mental.' I walk out at that. I can't listen to any more. I'd rather shut myself away in my room.

Later that evening, once everything had calmed down, I appealed to my dad, but he backed up Loony Tunes Susannah, and yeah, OK, she's his wife, but I am his daughter. And I called Mum, and even she said that I have to listen to Nicholas and Susannah because they know where I should and shouldn't go.

The grounding for one week stands and to be honest I wouldn't care, only it includes Saturday and that rules out Aaron's party. Everyone's going – everyone apart from me – and I promised I'd go. Maddy will flip.

All week I do as I'm told, arriving home early from college. I swim, do my homework and help out, setting the table for Marie and carrying washing upstairs. I even take the dogs out, waiting patiently as they sniff every other fence, wall or lamp post.

Funny how I'm allowed to walk the dogs in the dark on a quiet spooky street, I think, as I take them for the third day in a row. I swear I'm in as much danger here where it's quiet and no one would see if I got mugged or worse. Mind you, no one would attack me while I'm with these evil-looking hounds. I reckon they'd tear anyone to shreds, not necessarily to protect me, maybe just for fun.

I bring them in via the back door and the boot room, expecting Susannah to be in the kitchen or the snug, but there's only Marie preparing some wacko gluten-free raw snacks.

'Where's Susannah?' I ask, disappointed she's not there to see I've walked the dogs (without being asked).

'She not here. She go book club.'

This is bad news. Susannah's gone for hours on book club nights and she always comes back tipsy, which makes me wonder if books are really the point.

'So, I take it Susannah's not eating with us?'

'No eat tonight,' Marie says.

'Any chance we can have something normal?'

Marie smiles, and says, 'Alicia want chicken. I make Filipino style. You like?'

I do like chicken Filipino style, as do Alicia and Nicholas (who, under strict instructions from Susannah, arrives home early). Marie says the chicken is "adobo" and whatever that means, it's banging.

'Dad, you know how you love me?' I say, as we're sat at the table, 'well, there's this party on Saturday and I've been looking forward to it for ages.'

Nicholas looks askance. 'Why are you telling me?'

'I really want to go and Susannah won't let me.'

'You know you're putting me in an awkward position right now.'

'Everyone's going. I'm the only one not allowed. You're treating me like a little kid. I'm nearly eighteen.' He's non-committal although he does agree to "broach the subject" with Susannah.

'That's like asking a favour from Cruella de Vil.'

'She has your best interests at heart.'

'What about my mental well-being? Because I won't feel good if I'm left out – who would?' It's an angle I know, and he smiles like he finds that amusing and I think, fingers crossed, it'll work.

But it turns out the answer's no because apparently, 'One has to make decisions and stick to them, otherwise the lesson isn't learnt. Children must have a clear understanding of boundaries.'

'I'm not a child.'

'You're seventeen – legally you are a child,' Susannah says. 'Sometimes, and you will understand this one day, one has to be cruel to be kind. It's the only way the message sinks in.'

'It's so unfair. You're being ridiculous!' I storm out and slam the door, but it doesn't make me feel any better. What does help though is the way I roll up my black dress, stuff make-up in a backpack and sneak out while Susannah's out with the dogs on Saturday afternoon.

I turn off my phone and go straight to Maddy's.

# TWENTY-SIX

As usual Maddy has a free yard (Mr and Mrs Costa are out at their shop), so the first thing we do is raid the drinks cupboard, siphoning off vodka.

'Want some now?' Maddy asks even though it's three o'clock in the afternoon. 'We can take it slow.' She grins because we both know we won't do that. And we take over the family computer, posting videos on YouTube.

'Do a proper one,' Maddy says, 'sing something.'

'Like what?'

'I don't know, surprise me.'

I sing the first song that comes to mind: *Will You Still Love Me Tomorrow* – thinking Amy Winehouse as well as Carole King and The Shirelles, because I love all of them.

Maddy films me like she always does and we upload it to YouTube and Facebook. 'That'll show Gabriel Walker what he's missing,' she says, and I want to say something, explain how it is (and how happy I am now we're back together), but I don't know how, and so I just push it to the back of my mind because I know the chance will come later on and I'm sure she'll be fine with it, although she does say, 'Promise me you won't get back with him.' And I fudge the issue by shrugging and saying, 'That it would be a weird thing to promise.'

We help ourselves to more vodka from the cupboard and get changed and do our hair and make-up. Maddy also has a black dress, but as she's bigger her dress appears tight. 'That's a proper cleavage you've got there, girl,' I say.

'My best feature – no, actually I like my teeth best. They're so straight.' She smiles at herself in the mirror, and I'm taken aback. I've never thought her teeth that great. Yes, they're straight but they're wide and chunky like tabs of sugar-free gum.

'You've got great hair,' I say. It's long, thick and chestnut brown. 'And eyebrows.'

'Eyebrows?' She flicks her hair over one shoulder. And I don't know why but I'm in such a party mood that I sing OutKast's *Hey Ya!* and we dance.

'You're so good. That is such a tune, hope they play that later,' she says. 'How will you feel if Gabe goes with someone else tonight?'

'I haven't thought about it,' I say, because why would I when we're secretly back together?

'Would it bother you though?'

'He won't,' I say, almost giving it away.

'Yeah, but would you mind?'

I shrug. 'It's not like I own him.'

'So, you'll be all right with it? I mean he's bound to get with someone. He's good-looking and he's always been like that.'

'What do you mean?'

'I never said before, but we were sort of in a thing at one point.'

What is she getting at? I study her closely. 'When was that?' I ask, annoyed that she's even talking about Gabe.

'Way back, long before you arrived.'

'That's all right then,' I say, through gritted teeth. 'What exactly went on?'

She continues to look in the mirror, concentrating as she applies thick eyeliner. 'Oh, you know, the usual, we used to always get together at parties.'

'Nothing serious then,' I say.

'What is serious?' She stops applying her make-up and meets my eye as I stare at her reflection in the mirror and I'm wondering if I really know her at all.

Aaron lives on the Woodville estate in a flat on the third floor of a block called Friston House. We get the bus and sit at the back. We're barely talking. There's too much going around my head.

'You're in a great party mood,' she says.

I stare out the window as the bus turns off the main road past large houses, a school, a park and a pub.

'This could be it coming up,' she says. 'D'you know where to get off?'

'Carina knows, call her.'

Carina's meeting us there because she lives nearby.

'Hi, hun,' Maddy says, 'we're on the bus. Where do we get off?' There's silence for a moment as she listens. 'We just passed a row of shops. I can see blocks of flats.' Maddy rings the bell, and we disembark on the edge of a brightly lit estate.

'There's loads of blocks of flats.' I look for signs.

Maddy increases her pace. She's either desperate to get there, desperate to escape me or nervous due to the neighbourhood.

'Are you worried?' I ask, as I lag behind. 'You're getting like Susannah.'

'Keep moving, we'll find it.'

'It looks like they're decorating.' There are roadside skips and the ground-floor railings have signs saying "Wet Paint". 'Can you slow down a bit? I can't go so fast with my ankle.'

'Ugh. I keep forgetting you're disabled.'

'Love you too.' I continue at my own pace. 'That one says "Friston".' There are large yellow letters fixed to the end wall of the second block.

At the door Maddy buzzes up to gain access, and makes for the grubby-looking lift.

I pull a face. 'I'm not going up in that pissy lift. It stinks.'

'You'll take ages on the stairs.'

I shrug. 'Take the lift if you like, I'm walking.' I open the door to the stairwell and Maddy follows. I'm slow but eventually we make our way up the three flights to a balcony walkway that leads to Aaron's front door. I pause to check the view, looking away from Maddy towards the river and buildings beyond. There are a thousand tiny lights. It's magical like Christmas or Disneyland or a star-filled galaxy.

Maddy raps on the door and Carina opens it like she's been waiting for us. 'Maddy, Ren.' We hug. 'Glad you're here. It's pretty dead.'

'No Idris?' Maddy asks, as we both know that's why she thinks it's dead.

She pouts. 'Not yet – not sure he's coming. He says it's a kids' party.'

'His loss,' I say, 'anyhow, there's always Ross.'

'Is he coming?'

'I don't know, probably. I had to turn off my phone – avoiding the step-monster.'

Carina laughs. 'Is that what you're calling her now?'

'She's getting stupidly strict, like I'm in danger at all times.'

'She cares,' Maddy says, 'you're lucky. It could be far worse.'

In the living room people are standing in groups drinking. Aaron, who's by the iPod dock sorting a playlist, takes a moment's break to welcome us. 'My favourite girls.' He kisses us. 'Drinks are through there.'

In the small galley kitchen there are bottles lined up on the work surface.

'Cheeky little cider, ladies?' says a lad who's acting as bartender.

'I prefer vodka. Make it a large one, thanks.' I find a couple of plastic cups.

'I don't recognise you – you not at Cam's?'

'We're at Bourne's.'

'Still at school then.' He laughs at his own joke. 'I'm Omar, by the way, and you are?'

'Ren.'

'I know that name. You're seeing my bro, Gabe – I play football with him.'

'She *was* seeing him.' Maddy sounds happy that she thinks it's over.

While he looks at me quizzically and says, 'I thought…'

I don't let him finish. 'Thanks for the drink, see you around.' I head back to the other room where Calvin Harris is on the sound system and Aaron's waving his arms singing *Ready for the Weekend.* He gestures for us to join him but I resist, keen to drink more before I dance.

'You can't turn down the birthday boy,' Holly Appleby says, and she briefly dances with him.

The small living room fills up and Aaron returns. 'Ren, loving your look tonight.' He takes my hand and pulls me towards the middle of the room. 'Come on, cut some shapes, give it some.'

He gyrates in an over-the-top way, and I twerk as a joke, and I'm not sure when exactly Gabriel arrives as I'm too busy laughing as Aaron dances behind me, thrusting as he pretends to smack my arse.

Carina squeezes my arm, and mouths "Gabriel".

I straighten up, smile and wave, but Gabriel looks away, while Maddy, who's talking to James, looks over with a raised eyebrow.

Aaron heads to the kitchen. Meanwhile, there's confusion near the iPod dock. 'Quick, put the TV on,' Fenton says. Someone's spilt drink on the dock and it's no longer working. Ross finds a music channel and turns the volume up high in the hope Aaron won't notice.

'Gabriel keeps looking over,' Carina says. 'He still likes you, I know it.'

And I want to talk to him, but I sense it's not going to be easy, so instead I drink. Meanwhile Maddy's with James, who has his hand in his belt like a cowboy, which makes Carina giggle. But Maddy's looking everywhere but at him.

We down our drinks and go for refills and hang in the kitchen.

More lads arrive – a large group I don't recognise. They're wearing labels, expensive stuff most of us can't afford.

'Who are they?' I ask Carina, as I knock back another drink.

'I dunno.'

'I think I'm going to be sick.' Nausea hits me without warning.

'That was quick,' Carina says. 'Did you drink loads before you came out?' She guides me to the bathroom and holds my hair out of the way. 'This is all about Gabe, isn't it? Just talk to him. He's crazy about you, I know it.'

'I can't. It's awkward. He thinks I was flirting with Aaron.'

'It was obvious you were messing about. He looks unhappy.'

'He's pissy with me and he'll say something horrible. And I can't deal with that – not from him. It would kill me.'

'He still likes you, I know it – he wouldn't be staring otherwise.'

'I don't know.' I sigh, because, yes, he did still like me until he saw me dancing with Aaron and now it's all complicated again.

I splash water on my face and Carina takes me to the kitchen and makes me drink loads of water. 'I'm all right. I'm fine.'

Carina's face lights up like she's been given a puppy. *Idris?*

I turn around and sure enough he's there. 'I'll leave you to it.' I sway my way back into the living room and stop abruptly. At the far side, beyond people dancing, Maddy's talking to Gabe. My insides twist. *What is she doing?*

I can hardly bear it, but I want to know. Maddy's looking up at Gabe and talking intently, and worst of all, he's listening.

I go back to the kitchen. I want to talk to Carina but she's with Idris. Should I butt in? I don't know. I glance around looking for an alternative.

'Are you lost?' someone says. He's tall, dark, good-looking, with a stud in his ear that may or may not be a diamond.

'Aren't we all,' I reply, as if it's some deep existential question. I don't need this, he's not Gabe, I think and move away before he can ask anything else.

What now? I scan the room, and thankfully Idris goes off to the toilet.

'Carina?'

She smiles, and gives me a hug. 'You OK?'

'Did anything ever happen between Maddy and Gabe?' I say, immediately wishing I hadn't dared ask.

Carina looks upwards as she tries to remember. 'Year Nine, I think they may have kissed – truth or dare at the skatepark, but then again we all kissed.'

'Is that it?' I want to laugh, but I can't because I know Gabe's being funny with me and it's unfair and I'm so upset.

She shrugs. 'They may have kissed at a party one time, but nothing really. It's you he likes. It's obvious.' Idris returns, so I head back to the other room where there in the shadows Maddy remains talking with Gabe.

*What the hell*, I take a deep breath and go over. 'Hi,' I say, and swallow hard.

Maddy looks around. There's no smile.

'I need to talk to Gabe,' I say in a way that makes it clear she should go.

She shrugs and backs off slowly, while his expression is serious. 'Hi,' he says.

'Are you ignoring me?' I ask.

'I said "Hi", didn't I?'

'You seem annoyed. Is something wrong?'

His eyes are hard. 'Are you making out you don't know? You were dancing and flirting with Aaron – it was completely out.'

'It wasn't serious. We were only messing about.'

'He's my mate.'

'It was nothing, just a laugh.'

'I don't get why you were dancing with him?'

'It wasn't like proper dancing.'

'I wouldn't dance with your mates, not like that, it's disrespectful.'

'No one knows we're back together.'

'So you can flirt with anyone?'

'I wasn't flirting.'

'Looked like that to me.'

'You're being ridiculous.'

'Yeah, you reckon? D'you know what he's like?'

'He's OK as a mate.'

'He uses girls, treats them like dirt.'

'It was just a dance. We were mucking about.'

'That's not how it looked.'

'It was nothing. What about you chatting with Maddy the whole time when you've got history?'

He snorts with laughter. 'Are you mad?'

'Isn't there something you need to tell me?'

'I don't get what you mean.'

'Maddy?' I say, like that's all I need to say.

'What about her?'

'You had a thing going?'

'No.' He shakes his head.

'Are you sure about that?'

Gabe rolls his eyes. 'Are we talking Year Nine? I was, what, fourteen?'

Maddy's on the far side. She says something to Aaron and he comes over.

My body tenses. *What the hell is he going to say? Don't make it worse.*

'Guys, what's the beef? You're ruining the vibe,' Aaron says. 'It's my eighteenth and you lot are spoiling it. If you really have to argue, take it outside.'

He wouldn't even have noticed without Maddy getting involved.

'We can talk on the balcony.' I nod towards the front door and walk ahead, checking behind to ensure Gabe's following.

Weird – it all started with that kiss on the balcony at the boat club at Holly Appleby's party and now it looks like it's about to end on a concrete balcony outside Aaron's flat – but not before I've fought for it a whole lot more.

'You've got it all wrong,' I say. 'I'd never go off with any of your mates or anyone else.' He looks towards the furthest block of flats with its random pattern of glowing windows and I imagine all the people in each and every one of those flats is happier than me right now. 'Is that it then? It's all over?' My ankle hurts and I grip the metal railing as I take the weight off my ankle. 'That moved a bit,' I say, 'that's not safe.' I shift further along.

Gabe stares into the distance and I feel like crying. 'Can you just answer me because you're making me feel crap and I haven't even done anything wrong.'

'It looked like you're into him.'

'He's an idiot. You know I've always thought that.'

'He's always liked you.'

'I can't help that.'

He turns towards me, and there's a small movement in his neck as he swallows. 'It was just a laugh – you were messing about?'

I nod. 'Nothing in it. I don't like Aaron – never have – it's you.'

His eyes soften slightly.

'I'm not interested in anyone but you. You know that.'

He swallows again, and looks at the ground, and I reach out and take his hand and he lets me, turning his body towards me.

'I'm sorry,' I say, 'if it looked wrong, but really, honestly, it was nothing.'

I move closer, pressing my body into him, and he lets me

although he doesn't respond. Instead, he looks outwards, away from me and into the far distance beyond all the other flats and as far as the eye can see.

I wrack my brain, trying to think how I can reach him and make it all right, while out of the corner of my eye I see a flicker of movement.

'Shit,' he says under his breath, and my heart thumps as I think our relationship's about to go from bad to worse, but it's not about me. Gabe's staring down, over the balcony while taking care not to be seen. There's a group of lads following the concrete path that leads to the block's main door.

'Who are they?' I ask, as flashes of Susannah-type fears fill my head: gangs, drugs, knives, guns, rape – whatever you do, never go on an estate.

'It's Jamil and his mates. I need to warn Aaron.'

'What?' Gabe leaves me, and dashes back to Aaron's door and disappears inside. What should I do? I stand frozen, thinking I should follow but I'm queasy and the fresh air helps. Are they really heading this way? If I stay a little longer, I'll find out and I can run back and let everyone know.

Two doors down, a front door is ajar. It opens a touch wider as a boy peeks out. He's cute, about three or four years old with curly black hair and large dark eyes. He's dressed only in a T-shirt and nappy.

'Hello,' I say and smile and wave and try to shoo him back inside. 'Bedtime.'

The boy's eyes widen with an expression of what? Confusion perhaps? I follow his eyeline. He's looking behind me. I turn to see who or what it is, while in the other direction Jamil and his pals arrive on the balcony, commenting like I'm the hottest babe in west London.

'Party's over. It's all winding down,' I say, and then for some reason my mind goes blank.

Something happened – a shock, a shift, an abrupt change – I'm aware there's a missing moment or moments, like you get the morning after the night before.

My head throbs. There's a haziness – a fog of confusion – what is it?

What happened?

How drunk am I or was I?

There is someone, at least one person.

Conversation breaks down.

Something is said/was said and that something is so ridiculous that I laugh – am laughing – swaying – drunk and nauseous – and something or someone overreacts.

I feel a weight. A shove.

I've been hit, or was I pushed?

I sense petulance and frustration – my laughing face in rictus as I double over the balcony's metal safety rail. It presses into my waist, saving me … until it gives way.

I fall – am falling – and seconds stretch like blown glass as I pass the glowing yellow street lamps and the balcony below.

Head first, I go down screaming, past windows, railings and more windows as rising up to meet me … there's concrete.

# TWENTY-SEVEN

Will you ever rest? Lionel asks, his voice weary. I'd like to say good morning to you but I fear that for you there is no such thing.

*Good morning, Lionel,* I say. My head's pounding, as it does at the start of each and every day. *I've got the worst headache.*

Don't we all, my dear.

*This is different – worse than you can imagine, like it's been smashed.*

Migraine perhaps?

*I fell on my head.*

Oh?

*My death day, you wanted to know?*

You're ready to talk about it?

*It is all about me – I'm a self-obsessed teenager, remember?*

On reflection, I was a little unfair when I said that. Are you sure you want to talk about it?

*I think it might help.*

How did you fall?

I tell him the whole sorry story, going right back to my first day at Bourne's even though I fear such great detail might bore him. He doesn't interrupt – not once. And when I reach the end where everything stops, only it doesn't and I carry on dead-but-alive just like Lionel – I don't need to explain. He knows.

There's silence, apart from the noise of a plane overhead.

The river flows, while ducks sleep in the reeds.

I wait for Lionel's response.

He's quiet for a moment, and then says, I am so very sorry to hear all this. What a terrible, shocking and indeed painful end. I feel for you, I really do.

The sky's a cold light blue with fluffy white clouds like the ones kids draw.

*Funny how we're not up there*, I say.

You never believed all that, did you?

*I wanted to when I was little.*

There's one thing you haven't said – indeed your story is somewhat confused – who was it that pushed you? I take it you were pushed?

I think only of the eyes, that's all I can envision.

*I don't have a clear memory*, I tell Lionel. *I remember the eyes, the look of them, the intent – it was all there in that split second and I know that at that precise moment I knew who it was, but for some reason it's gone.*

You can't remember?

*I did fall on my head.*

A severe blow to the head can certainly cause amnesia.

*The thing is I know that I know. I just can't retrieve it.*

You may have blanked out the memory because it's too painful.

*It will come back to me though, won't it?*

It's possible. Memories can be triggered by the smallest of things: the smell of a particular perfume for instance or the sound of a favourite song. But these are senses that belong to the living. For us I cannot be sure.

*Well, whatever, it's not like the police can interview me for clues.*

Indeed. Our voices are rarely heard.

*This must be why I go over it all night after night. I need to retrieve what it is that I already know. Somehow I must access that knowledge I've buried deep inside.*

A skanky brown dog approaches.

*Go away*, I tell it, and for once a dog does as I say.

Ren, forgive me, but I have to ask: Gabriel was with you on the balcony that night and yet you are wholly convinced he was not the cause of your demise?

His words make me reel. *It wasn't Gabe*, I say, my voice choked.

I'm sorry. I didn't mean to upset you.

*Gabe had nothing to do with it. I told you that.*

How can you be so sure?

*Lionel, how can you even ask that? It's in the eyes. That look, the one I remember, Gabe never looked like that. He never could or would. He loves me.*

He's been charged.

*They've got it wrong.*

I do have faith in the English justice system. If they have the wrong man, then I'm sure the situation will be rectified.

*How can someone like Gabe be in prison? It's ridiculous.*

Are you sure that he is?

*He hasn't visited me. If he were out, he'd come straight here – for definite.*

If he knows you're here. My dear, as I've said before, you need to break through.

*Easier said than done.*

People hear you.

*Yeah, mad old men and little kids.*

Give it time.

*I haven't got time. The trial could be any day now.*

A steady stream of commuters walks past. There's a well-dressed young woman in a camel coat, short stripy skirt and knee-high leather boots, her blonde hair in a ponytail. She works in fashion, I reckon. There's a group of three: two men in hoodies and anoraks and a plump lady – call centre workers perhaps? And there's a man in his fifties in a black padded coat, smart trousers and leather brogues – solicitor, surveyor, bank manager?

*Is this all there is? Will I only wait and watch the world go by while nothing happens to me ever again?*

There's no need for that kind of talk, Lionel says. You're a girl on a mission, remember that.

*I'm a girl who let her life be taken – pushed over a balcony onto concrete. I should have been able to save myself.*

One mustn't think like that. I don't believe for a minute anyone would have seen that coming.

*Has anything similar happened to you? I don't mean murder of course, because I know you died of old age.*

Boredom, I died of boredom, my dear, one must get it right. There is nothing interesting about how my life ended.

*It's better that way.*

Boredom has its relative advantages, but to answer your question, yes and no.

*What does that mean?*

I mean I wasn't so great myself, but at the same time there were people who weren't so great to me.

*You know it's ages since I heard anything new and it's definitely your turn so come on, you must tell me everything. It's only fair.*

Oh, very well, I may as well get it over with. As I've mentioned before, I inherited a small bakery from my father that I expanded to include a tearoom and a formal function room, where I catered for christenings, weddings and wakes. It was a good little business. We did outside catering and delivered cakes and pastries throughout west London.

I worked extremely hard, as I'd watched my parents work hard before me, and that led me to conclude that it was no business for a woman. I wanted my wife, Isobel, to have the luxury of staying at home and looking after our children.

*She was happy to stay at home?*

She was.

*How many children did you have?*

Just the one – Janet came along in 1941. We wanted more but it wasn't to be.

*I'm sorry.*

I always wanted a son. I adored Janet of course, but I wanted someone to carry on the business.

*Couldn't Janet do that?*

It was different in those days. Running a bakery, tearoom and function room, not to mention the outside catering and deliveries, it was hard with long, unsociable hours. I'd watched my own mother work long hours and she was often overtired and had little energy left for me. I didn't want that for Isobel or Janet, but looking back I'd say that I may have been wrong.

Work gives a person purpose – as does rearing a child of course – that goes without saying, but as the child matures, the mother's role lessens in practical ways and that's when a lack of purpose can become problematic.

*What do you mean?*

We grew apart. I was working all hours to grow the business to secure our future prosperity while Isobel stagnated. She lost herself. It was as if the lively, bright girl I met who had a good brain and a decent admin job, well, it was as if her brain turned to mush. Perhaps she was depressed, and I'm not proud of myself for saying this but I found her trivial and uninteresting, and worse I'd employed someone new, a young woman who was everything Isobel was not.

*Ah right, OK, I know where this is going.*

It's not easy for me to share this. You will think less of me.

*I'm not going to judge you.*

Sometimes it can't be helped.

*What was the new girl called?*

Maxine. She was a sweet, capable lady with a good heart.

*She knew you were married? That's well out. She should have stayed away. How old was she?*

She was about twenty-four, as I remember. It's a terrible cliché I know – a middle-aged man going to seed thinking a younger woman is the answer.

*So, what happened?*

It was a foolish dalliance; perhaps I momentarily lost my mind.

Well, that's my excuse, but I did care for her. It hurt terribly.

*But you stayed with Isobel?*

Yes, I did.

*How long did it last with Maxine?*

It was about eighteen months.

*That's a long time.*

To you it would seem long, but to someone who eventually clocked up forty years of marriage, eighteen months was a mere weekend away.

*Your "dalliance" must have been pretty full on?*

Like I said, I cared for her very much.

*What happened?*

We were found out, and by Janet of all people. She was about fourteen at the time. Can you imagine what damage I must have caused? I considered the bakery my domain and although I was discreet, I assumed I was safe to carry on as I wished. Janet popped in one day after school. She never did that and to this day I don't know what made her come in to see me then, but she did, and as she was my daughter she felt no need to knock on my office door.

*Oh no.*

I am eternally ashamed.

*She told Isobel?*

To my even greater shame I attempted to bribe Janet to keep quiet. Initially she went along with it but her conscience got the better of her.

*She told her mum?*

Yes, it was terrible. I don't suppose you even know what it's like to realise you've truly hurt someone.

*It wasn't great how I walked out on my mum and stuff.*

You were so hurt you ran as far as you could from that awful boy who upset you in Devon. You, my dear, have lived a good and blameless life.

*Lionel, you're upsetting me now.*

One should tread lightly on this earth, and that is what you've done.

*How did Isobel react?*

I can still see her face – the disappointment – she appeared crushed. She cried for hours, begging me to give up Maxine.

*What did you do?*

Maxine stimulated my mind. She was interested in many things: current affairs, art, music. She was in touch with the world and everything that was going on. It was as if she had her finger on the pulse of London.

*What was she doing stuck in a bakery then?*

She ran the functions: christenings, weddings, etc. It wasn't easy. We were fully booked. The job was hard work and she did it well. I didn't want to lose her. We went away to Brighton for the weekend, predictable I know and I felt such terrible, all-consuming guilt. That's when I knew I had to end it.

*How were things after that?*

There are always consequences. Janet never really forgave me. I was diminished in her eyes and rightly so. She became very protective of her mother.

*And Isobel?*

She was a stoical sort. There were tears, but after a few weeks she never mentioned it again. I was extremely grateful for this approach. However, years later she developed breast cancer and I've always blamed myself.

*How could that be your fault?*

She bottled up her emotions. All the hurt and pain I caused had to go somewhere.

*That doesn't seem scientifically sound to me, Lionel.*

It's a hunch. Three years she battled on. She was sixty-one when she passed.

*I'm sorry.*

So am I, she deserved better.

*You're too hard on yourself.*

We're all products of our own upbringings to a certain extent and we often react against how we were brought up.

*I didn't really get the chance to do that.*

I'm sorry, it must be both painful and irritating for you to hear how I cocked up my many chances to live a good and useful life.

*I don't take your relatively long lifespan personally, Lionel.*

It gets worse. My daughter later married a man called Tony. They met at work. She was a trainee accountant and he worked in credit control. I liked Tony. We talked football and cricket and I was pleased when they settled down.

Tony was a man I could work with, someone I could trust. I wanted to get him involved in the business so I took him on board and gradually gave him more responsibility, and then when Isobel was first diagnosed I took that as a sign for me to step down.

*See, you're a good bloke. You did the right thing by her in the end.*

Ren, I signed the whole business over to Tony. How stupid can one man be? He later did the dirty on my daughter. And for the second time in her life she walked in on something no wife or daughter should ever have to see.

*That's raw.*

Yes, and Janet's nothing like Isobel, believe me. It was instant divorce. She didn't mess around.

*Did she have kids?*

One, a girl called Sally – apple of my eye.

*So, what happened to the business?*

It had to be sold and split fifty/fifty, but not before Tony siphoned off the profits and ran it into the ground. It broke my heart.

*Did Janet meet anyone else?*

There were a few gentlemen friends but I don't think she wanted to risk marrying again. It was hard for her to trust.

*And what about you after Isobel's death – did you remarry?*

No, I spent the last ten years of my life alone – I deserved that.

*So, did Janet order the bench?*

No, it wasn't Janet.

*Who was it?*

Ha, can't you guess?

*Not Maxine?*

No, I never heard from her again.

*Who then?*

Do you know what it says?

*You mean the metal thing?*

Yes, the inscription on the plaque.

*I've no idea.*

As I recall, it says: "In loving memory of Isobel Mathews, beloved wife and mother. She fought so bravely and lives forever in our hearts". And then below that I understand there's a separate plaque that goes something along the lines of: "Lionel Mathews, a lifelong local resident, he loved walking the Thames path," and there are the dates we were born and died, etc.

*Your bench is also Isobel's bench? Did you order it?*

Yes, as ludicrous as it may sound, I ordered the damn bench.

*Did you expect to be commemorated alongside Isobel?*

No, it never occurred to me. I wanted only to honour her.

*How come she's not here?*

She has no reason to be. She's at rest.

*But you're not.*

Well, I wasn't to begin with anyway. I used to think it was about Janet or even Maxine – that things were left unsaid. But perhaps it was more about me. I think I needed to forgive myself.

*Your daughter Janet – does she visit?*

She has done, but not for a good while.

*How long?*

You know I'm not so good with time, but the last visit was a while before Norman went. She may have moved house or be unwell. She'll be in her seventies now. She could very well have passed away.

*She might be a bench.*

For her sake, I sincerely hope that's not the case.

*Yeah, I couldn't agree more – who wants to be a bench?*

# TWENTY-EIGHT

Two men approach. One is tall and thin and in his fifties while the other's of a similar age but seated on a red mobility trike. 'Let's stop here, Phil,' the man says, as he manoeuvres his trike to face the river.

'Bench is a bit damp.' Phil lays out his raincoat on the seat and sits down.

'At least the sun's shining for a change.' The man on the mobility trike leans back and closes his eyes as if to soak up some rays.

Phil smiles. 'Can't watch the river with your eyes closed, Mikey.'

'Just having a moment.' Mikey opens them. 'What a lovely spot this is – love weeping willows – my favourite tree.'

'I'm more of an oak man myself,' Phil says.

A huskie and its owner walks past, closely followed by a pointer, two black labradors and a cross-breed.

'So many dogs around here,' Mikey says.

'Should've brought ours.'

'I know, but it's difficult when we need to go shopping as well. You can walk them later.'

'I thought you'd say that.' Phil smiles as if he'd do anything for Mikey.

'Do you think you get kingfishers around here?' Mikey asks. 'I've never seen one. Can you believe that – fifty-five and never seen a kingfisher. Bet you get loads of foxes here at night. I'd love to camp out and watch them.'

'Bit cold for that,' Phil says.

'Yeah, maybe in the summer, eh.'

*I like foxes*, I say.

'I know you like foxes,' Mikey says.

'What?' Phil says.

*No, it's me, Lauren, the name on the bench, but I prefer to be called Ren.*

Mikey turns around in the seat of his mobility trike. 'Phil, shove over a bit – let me read that plaque?' He puts on his glasses. 'My God, it is Lauren 'n' all. We're going to have to go.'

'Why, what's up?'

'They're talking to me again.'

'Who are?'

'The dead – look at the plaque – Lauren, she's talking to me.'

'Really?' Phil doesn't look surprised. 'Do we have to go so soon? It's so lovely here. Surely you can ignore it.'

'Lauren, I don't know who you are or what you want, but I can't help you, love. I've got enough problems of my own.'

*Please*, I say, *I really need to talk to someone. You see, not many people can hear me. It's a rare thing. Please, just a few minutes?*

His face drains of colour. 'It's no good, she's begging me and I can't deal with it right now. Come on, Phil, shift it, we're out of here.'

Phil gathers up his raincoat and they move on.

*Typical.*

Good work, Ren, Lionel says.

I sigh. *Even when I do break through they don't want to know.*

# TWENTY-NINE

Beneath a blank white sky, they arrive like a murder of crows to gorge on the poor, pathetic corpse that is the generally accepted version of me, my life and how it ended.

*You're wrong, all of you. Go away. It's Gabriel I want.*

My dad, Nicholas, leads the black-clad procession as it approaches. Nicholas Miller: banker, triathlete, Simple Minds fan. Where were you for most of my life? How come we only had a few months and that even then you barely showed? I guess you thought we had all the time in the world.

It's like the first time we met – you kept me waiting for hours, stuck talking to Susannah when all I wanted was you. She's already waited seventeen years, what are a few more hours? Is that what you thought? What was the hold-up? Were you scared?

I remember it clearly – how you arrived gone ten – hammered you were, and even so my first impression was that you were pretty cool for an old guy: tall, slim and dressed in a dark suit. 'Where is she?' I heard you say, before you filled the doorway of the snug. It was like a TV show reunion with smiles and a big hug like you didn't want to let go. I was emotional, felt myself well up instantly and that was freaky as I had no idea that deep down there was something missing, a big empty space aching for a dad, my dad, you. It was a role I needed filled. And I thought I'd found you and that it would be sorted. We'd spend loads of time, get to know each other – only it didn't happen. You're never there. What do you do? Who do you hang out with? Someone must get the best of you, I just don't know who. Perhaps you have a Maxine? That would be raw. Susannah doesn't deserve that.

'This is it,' Nicholas gestures towards the bench, and then stands back so that everyone can see.

Mum, Jay and Mum's boyfriend Billy press forward. They've brought Nanna up from Devon. Jay and Billy each have hold of one of her arms to prop her up.

'It's smashing,' Nanna says, 'what a lovely spot.'

'Here, Mum, you sit on the end there.' Mum helps Nanna sit at one end so that she doesn't obscure the plaque.

*Where's Alicia?* I ask.

I see her with Susannah – standing well back.

*Come closer, little sis.*

Carina, Idris and Maddy step forward. Carina has a new beanie and a thick wool scarf that she's repeatedly wound around her neck. She looks down, her bottom lip quivers and Idris takes her hand. 'Be strong, Cas,' he says.

Maddy reads the plaque. 'She hated being called Lauren.'

Carina shrugs. 'Parents always like your proper full name.'

Alicia edges closer, dark shadows beneath her eyes.

*I miss you, little sis.*

Her face pales and her eyes are wide as she turns away and finds Grandma Judy, who is as always looking regal in a smart fur-trimmed grey coat, black court shoes and matching handbag. She's with Holly Appleby, probably talking about her ballet days and how she once danced with Rudolf Nureyev. 'Alicia, darling, your reading at the service was perfect,' Judy says. 'I'm so proud of you.'

Aaron, Fenton and Ross pause. 'It's proper smart,' Aaron says. 'It's not Ren though. She was alive, man. Benches are for old people.'

'I hear what you're saying, but it's somewhere to go – I don't want to forget, if you know what I mean,' Fenton says.

'It don't make sense,' Aaron says. 'Whenever I think about it, I think no way was it Gabe. I don't buy that. He'd never hurt anyone.'

'You can't talk about that here, not now.' Ross points his phone at the code and opens the website that lights up with my name and the set of embarrassing kiddy photos followed by the film of me in that black dress singing Amy Winehouse's *You Know I'm No Good.*

'Listen to that voice,' Fenton says. 'She was good, man.'

Holly Appleby comes over. 'That was my eighteenth. What a party, do you remember? She blew everyone away.'

People gather round: college friends, and Mum, Jay, Nanna, Susannah, Dad, Alicia, Judy, Marie, Maddy, Carina and Idris. They all look sad. The wrong thing's happened to someone too young. That's how it is, some of us don't make it.

*Hey, thanks for coming, guys, good to see you.*

Grandma Judy shivers and folds her arms, while Alicia hugs herself. One by one, people close their coats tighter as if a harsh bitter wind has blown in.

*Hey, listen up, everyone, it wasn't Gabriel. If you love me, you'll help him.*

Judy looks bemused as she holds her hat, even though there is no gale, not even a breeze. 'What is it?' she says. 'It's turned dreadfully cold all of a sudden.'

*Alicia, tell everyone it wasn't Gabe – he's not like that.*

Alicia buries her head in her gran's armpit, her face hidden and a mitten blocking her other ear.

*Alicia, hear me now, I love you, little sis. Please listen, don't be scared. It wasn't Gabe. I know that for sure.*

Alicia is shaking, her small frame quakes and Judy struggles to contain and console her. She seeks out Dad, while keeping Alicia close to her side.

'This child is distraught,' Judy says. 'I'm taking her home.'

*Please, Alicia, don't be scared, it's only me.*

Alicia, my sweet little sister, my one true connection here today, my hope, walks away with Grandma Judy's arm around her while Dad, Mum, Jay, Billy and Susannah remain at the bench, thanking everyone for coming.

'Not long till the court case now,' Susannah says, touching Mum's arm.

'I'm so apprehensive about it,' Mum says. 'It's at the Old Bailey.'

Dad nods. 'All the most serious cases are tried there.'

'You'll stay with us for the duration of the trial, won't you, Annie?' Susannah says. 'I won't hear of you staying anywhere else.'

Mum looks away, her eyes hard as stone. 'It makes me so mad,' she says. 'Even here today I can't help thinking about that evil boy and what he did.'

*Mum, you're wrong. It wasn't Gabe. I'm so tired of saying it. Please listen.*

Who was it, Ren? Lionel asks. Try to remember.

All I can think of is Gabriel handcuffed and shoved into a prison van and taken to the Old Bailey – frustrated, frightened and flanked by security guards. He'll be alone in the dock without the money to pay for a decent lawyer. He doesn't stand a chance. *Lionel, I'm so upset. It's so unfair. Why don't they realise?*

Don't give up, my dear, let's try and break through together.

*How?*

What do you most want to say?

*It wasn't Gabe.*

Let's say it together – one, two, three:

*It wasn't Gabe*, we shout. *It wasn't Gabe.*

The mourners wrap their coats tighter, and quickly disperse.

# THIRTY

Rain falls daily with occasional breaks. At sunrise, the sky turns pink and mauve, but it doesn't last. Every day it rains and the river breaks its banks and water overflows onto the path, pooling at the feet of the bench.

*It's never-ending*, I say to Lionel.

Biblical, he says, never seen rain like it. In the past, people would have viewed such horrendous weather as a portent of worse to come.

*It's to do with the trial, I reckon. It must be soon.*

No one visits. Why would they? Commuters rush past, as do mums on the school run, pensioners, cyclists – everyone.

*Nobody stops here any more, not even Susannah. We've been abandoned.*

Weren't your family going away somewhere? Lionel says.

I think back to the day Alicia came with Dad, Susannah and Judy.

*You're right, they're on holiday: they've gone skiing.*

There you are then, no one's forgotten you. It's only old farts like me who are forgotten.

*Lionel, I don't believe anyone could ever forget you.*

The days become weeks with nothing but rain and the path regularly floods.

*The world's ended and we're the last to know.*

It wouldn't matter much if it had, Lionel says, not to us anyway.

*Speak for yourself. If the world's ended then I've lost all hope of ever seeing Gabe – that matters to me.*

I apologise, that was thoughtless. It matters to me also. I'd love for Gabriel to come. I'd very much like to meet him.

*Do you feel it?* I say.

You mean the damp?

*Yes.*

It's a phantom sense, like all that we see, think and feel. We are no more real than the measurement that is time.

*Time exists.*

Life exists; time merely attempts to package it.

Rain falls in heavy lines to merge with the brown river water that flows faster than usual. And I'd cry if I could, stuck here in the wet and the wind watching the trees flail and people rush past.

Rain falls, dogs visit, days pass.

And then finally there is sunshine: warming, golden, almost forgotten.

I stretch out, eyes closed, feel the warmth on my skin – only I don't. They're phantom feelings garnered from ancient memories of family holidays. Where did I go? France with Mum and Jay – Brittany – it was a disappointment. The weather was not much better than home. 'Why go abroad when we live next door to Cornwall?' Mum used to say. She was making the best of things, as she always does.

Saint Lucia, the Caribbean – that's where I was heading post-Christmas. Four days in Devon with Mum, Jay and Billy, then it was back to London to fly off with Dad, Susannah and Alicia for my first ever five-star luxury all-inclusive holiday. 'Even the sea is warm,' Susannah said, 'it's like a giant bath.'

'You'll love it,' Dad said. But I never got to find out.

Over the balcony I went, down, down in seconds that stretched to seem never-ending. The intensity of the impact smashed my skull and snapped most of my bones and squished my insides, while my heart remained intact, feeling only for Gabe as he yelled out – the sound that haunts me, alongside my own inner scream at myself for not realising that someone was out to get me and that my one true love was as lost to me as I was to him.

Fall from a height, they call it.

There was confusion and a man's voice, loud like he was talking on the phone. 'We've got a fall from a height – seventeen-year-old female – third-floor balcony, thirty-foot drop onto concrete.' They were all around me, dressed in green – emergency workers.

'Her name's Lauren, prefers to be called Ren,' a woman said.

They clamped big fat padded sponges to either side of my face and something sharp was put into the back of my hand. I vomited back onto myself and was choking – fingers were forced into my mouth. 'Airways clear,' a woman said, all matter of fact, like it wasn't life or death.

*Gabe?* 'I want Gabe,' I swear I said it, but no one took any notice. *Gabriel!*

'Can you move your feet for me, Ren?' the woman asked.

The pain had gone. I tried to look down.

'Can you wiggle your toes, Ren?'

'Let's take her in,' a man said.

The medics were all around me. 'One, two, three, lift,' a man said, and they shifted me onto a board.

*Gabe. I see him. Police are with him.*

'*Ren.*' He tried to reach me but they held him back.

*Gabe.*

He lashed out. And they gripped him, locked his arms and handcuffed him.

*Gabe.* I screamed.

A large, moon-face hovered over me – a woman with cropped hair. 'OK, Ren, we're about to lift you into the air ambulance. Have you been in a helicopter before? Well, don't worry, you're not alone, your friend Maddy's here to keep you company.' And I flew stretchered through the air into a small, red metal cave with straps everywhere and there was the grating, grinding noise of the helicopter's blades and engine.

'*I want Gabe.*' Someone squeezed my hand, and again I felt nauseous, as I lay there strapped flat and immobile.

I cried out, as did Gabriel. '*Ren*,' he shouted inside my head.

Then I was moving again, pinned flat to a trolley, bright lights above me and into an even brighter room.

A medic walked in. 'You must know that you are dying.' His voice was deep and actorly as if he were playing a part. *But how could he say that? Did he say that? Who is he?* I'd got it wrong. I knew it then. He was no medic…

I watched myself on the hospital bed below, aware that I had transitioned to energy. And it was as if I was looking through an old-fashioned viewfinder. The scene below was brilliantly lit while around me lay darkness.

'We're losing her,' a nurse said, her expression fraught, as she started chest compressions, pushing down with her whole weight.

Electrode pads were placed on my chest.

'Stand clear,' a man said, and a moment later he zapped me.

More chest compressions.

'Stand clear.'

Another shock.

More compressions.

Could they not hear the monitor's beep had flat-lined?

The nurse's eyes were wide.

'Come now, it's time,' the booming actorly voice said, and I knew that it was death. It would be a sweet release, I realised. The pain was so intense that I was willing to be taken away in every sense possible.

# THIRTY-ONE

Mum had to come to London a week before she had planned, a week before the weekend when we were going to shop and eat our way around the West End.

They laid me out ready in a room painted vomity beige.

The giant sponges had been taken away from either side of my face and I'd been cut open "to ascertain the exact physical cause of death". The lanky, know-it-all forensic pathologist knew I'd suffered severe head trauma, but didn't know enough to say who did it. Accident, misadventure or murder? The autopsy was inconclusive, stating only the obvious, death caused by blunt force trauma and multiple organ failure. And then I was stitched back up again as best he could.

'Can I touch her?' Mum asked, and the attendant said she could. So Mum leaned over and stroked my cold, still face, as hot tears welled in her eyes.

'My darling girl, I know it's you but it doesn't look like you.' She turned towards the attendant. 'My Ren was amazing, you see. She really was full of life. That's not her, it can't be. She's not there. She's gone.'

'I'm so sorry,' the woman said. 'This must be very hard.'

Of course it was hard. How could Mum equate this pale, lifeless corpse with me, and all my good and bad points?

'I know it's my daughter, but I can't see her there.' Mum turned away as if blocking out the sight of me might cancel out what had happened and bring me back to life. She looked back and I remained deathly still. She sighed heavily and peeled back the cloth from around my neck, and leant over. 'Is it at all possible – would you mind, I really need to see her tattoo?'

'Where is the tattoo?'

'It's on her upper back, at the top of her spine, below the base of her neck.'

With the help of a second attendant wearing plastic gloves, I was moved onto my side and momentarily held in that position so that Mum could see the tattoo she had never liked: a perfect permanently-inked life-size dragonfly.

Mum's finger traced over its four delicate wings. 'They don't live long, dragonflies,' Mum said, 'so beautiful and delicate and then in a short while they're gone – as if they're too special for this world.'

'That's a very pretty tattoo,' said the attendant, 'lovely colour.'

'Ultramarine blue – the most precious colour.'

I had told Mum that, just as Gabe had told me. Funny that she should repeat information from the person she believes killed me.

*You see, Mum, Gabe is all about good things. He was always building me up, making me feel special.*

# THIRTY-TWO

The funeral was in Devon. I hadn't been back since I left, and it wasn't the return I'd had planned. I'd been due to go at Christmas of course, but instead I arrived weeks early in the back of a blacked-out private ambulance, and spent a night in the chapel of rest at Coombes & Sons, the local undertakers. Mum visited late afternoon and placed one of my old teddy bears (what is it with her and bears?) in the coffin, alongside a note that I'll never get to read.

The following morning I was transferred to a hearse for the short journey uphill to the Church of St Peter, St Paul and St Thomas of Canterbury. I'd been there many times before with my primary school and we'd had to learn about its history. It was commissioned by a rich landowner called Sir William de Tracey to make up for the fact that he was involved in the murder of Thomas Becket in Canterbury Cathedral. Murderers are always there – in every age and at every level of society.

Anyway, back to me. The old stone church was packed, hundreds of people turned out – maybe I was as popular as Holly Appleby after all. But what a gloomy bunch… *Come on, guys, it happened weeks ago. Let's have a laugh.*

Kemi's eyes were red from the start. As soon as she was handed the order of service with its cover shot of me in that black lace prom dress, she was off, and it only got worse once she opened it up and saw a montage of snaps, including one of us joking about in badger hats on Haytor.

Eva Cassidy's *Songbird* played out on the sound system – a

beautiful song but enough to make anyone feel sad even on a good day. And would you believe Griff turned up. What did I ever see in that idiot? And he even brought Izzy along – *no more videos, please. I've seen enough of that girl.* Raven's College were at the back, and then there was the London crowd – *wonder what they think of Bovey?* Maddy, Carina, Idris, and even Holly with her blonde hair piled up in a messy bun on top of her head, and if she had applied eye make-up it had been rubbed away.

Aaron, Fenton, James and Ross were seated together. All my mates were there and then there were extra that I'd only ever considered as acquaintances. Everyone apart from Gabriel and back then I didn't know why. I thought something must have happened to him, like he'd been injured or was ill or had fallen out with his dad. I couldn't understand it and it ruined my day, and trust me, I'd been looking forward to it – it was all about me.

Family were at the front: distant relatives I'd not seen for years alongside Dad, Susannah, Alicia, Grandma Judy, Marie (Dad's housekeeper), and then there was Mum's partner Billy, Jay, Nanna and Mum.

*Dearest Mum*, I thought, as I watched her take the deepest breaths. Billy held her hand and Jay stroked her arm. *And how I wanted to put my arms around her and give her a big hug. Why didn't I do that more often? No point beating myself up about it. What's done is done. Only most people get a chance to rectify stuff – having years on me. It's only us truly young and prematurely deceased that don't get a second chance to make it right.*

It all got a bit heart-wrenching once it started. Kemi went up first and said, 'Ren was a great friend, the best you can have. She was always there for me and she could always make me laugh. We were founder members, and in fact the only members of the Badger Appreciation Society, even though we'd never seen a live badger despite our many attempts to track them around Bovey and on Dartmoor. Ren was, as we all know, an amazing singer. I checked her YouTube videos this morning and combined they've now had over 120,000 hits and I know that at least one record company has shown interest. Given the chance, Ren would have made it.' Kemi's voice cracked a little and she had to look away for a moment. 'I missed her from the moment she moved to London and now I miss her even more. She's gone, but will never be forgotten.' The last few words almost stuck in her throat, and Jay helped her back to her seat, her apple cheeks visibly streaked with tears.

It was his turn. 'Ren, my big sister, was always there for me. She walked me to school when I was little and she looked after me – especially when I was in trouble with Mum. She was always singing and I was usually trying to interrupt or muck up her recordings for a laugh. But that all changed when she won a talent contest on holiday in Cornwall when she was ten. She sang *Over the Rainbow*, and I couldn't believe it when all these people started crying. It was only then that I realised how good she was. Later on, it was karaoke and you couldn't get her off it. Singing was all she wanted to do and I'm gutted she never got the chance to follow her dream because she was the real deal, a proper star-in-waiting with a stellar talent that would have taken her far if only she'd got the chance.

'Ren, you'll always be my big sister and you'll always live on in our hearts and minds – remembered every hour of every day. We love you.'

Mum went up, her hands shaking. 'This is a poem called *She is Gone* by David Harkins.' She looked down at the piece of paper she was holding. There was silence, like she wasn't going to manage to read it out.

Billy stared, willing her to speak, as did everyone else.

She took the deepest breath like she needed all the oxygen available, and looked up and over the heads of everyone in the congregation, and recited the poem from memory, the last sweet words being, 'Smile, open your eyes, love and go on.'

Again, Jay stepped up and helped Mum back to her seat. Alicia, her hair in ringlets and dressed in a grey wool coat also read a poem called *Something Beautiful Remains*. And Susannah and even Holly Appleby all said a few words and really it was hard to believe they were talking about me.

Finally, Dad stepped up, his eyes downcast. '"What we have once enjoyed and deeply loved we can never lose, for all that we love deeply becomes a part of us." That quote from a lady called Helen Keller is particularly poignant for me. Ren arrived on my doorstep at a point in her life where she was finding herself. It was an honour to get to know her. I wish we'd had more time, but it wasn't to be and I can only be thankful for what we had. Ren, as we love you, so we miss you.'

Adele's version of the Bob Dylan classic *Make You Feel My Love* was played – enough to make anyone blub, and they carried me out to bury me deep in a freshly dug plot in the corner of the graveyard.

Only they didn't, because the corpse that once contained me had been left an empty shell as somehow I watched over it all: Nanna asking to remain in the church because seeing me committed to the earth would be too much for her, Mum's near collapse at the graveside halted only by Jay and Billy holding her up, Jay's failure to contain a loud wail as he sprinkled earth onto the coffin, Kemi's crumpled face, Alicia crying into Susannah's sleeve, and Carina leaning on Idris as Maddy dabbed at her eyes with a tissue and stared into the distance as my body was finally laid to rest – ready to rot to oblivion within the cold, damp, worm-filled earth.

# THIRTY-THREE

The trees hang heavy with blossom. Like giant pink powder puffs they stand further along the riverside behind the line of benches once jumped by Gabriel.

I see him now leaping from bench to bench until the space between them is too great and he falls and lies face down on the tarmac path, and I run to him, he rolls over, laughing, pulls me down and kisses me.

I loved that he was so spontaneous and free.

I'm thinking of him in the past tense? Is he completely lost to me?

At least the rain's gone for now. Spring is here with freakish warmth.

Isn't it glorious? Lionel says. *Oh, What A Beautiful Morning* – he sings the Howard Keel song that my Nanna loves and I join in and we laugh.

We're drying out in the heat, while couples and larger groups linger by the river to people-watch and enjoy the sun.

The air cools at dusk.

Today has been quite marvellous, Lionel says. The sun makes it almost worthwhile, don't you think? That warmth, we still have that.

*Yeah, it helps … a bit.*

The lamps light up and I know that I must let him retire to his own private thoughts. *Goodnight, Lionel. Rest in peace.*

Rest in peace, my dear.

Lionel becomes as silent as the wood of his bench and, as the riverside darkens I look forward to meeting Gabriel for the first time all over again.

I'm there at my first day at Bourne's, and then on to Chicken Shack, my heart beating fast at the mere sight of a boy so beautiful – *who is he? I have to know.* My heart races, as electrified by the sight of him as if it were the first time.

Only, there's a jolt, an interruption – the reliving instantly halted as I'm forced back to reality by a living, breathing presence at the bench.

*Why here?* I say. *There are loads of benches – four that way and nine the other, and that's not to mention all the others if you just keep walking further along. That would be great, thanks.*

It doesn't work. No one listens, but then I realise this person's come specifically to see me.

*Hello, you*, I say.

It's Maddy and she's brought someone I don't recognise. He's our age, tall, skinny with dark hair and heavy hooded eyes.

*Are you going to introduce me?*

Maddy flicks back her thick dark hair. She's wearing black leggings and a burgundy Harrington over a white T-shirt. She looks heavier.

*You've put on weight*, I say, without thinking, but it's OK because she didn't even hear me say hello.

Only Maddy does turn abruptly and stares, and I know that look. There's a bitter twist to her mouth. *Where and when have I seen that before?*

'This is the bench that's dedicated to that girl I was telling you about,' Maddy says to the guy.

'The murdered girl?' He doesn't seem very bright. 'What's she called?' He leans over and reads the plaque.

'Everyone called her Ren.'

Listen to that – she used the past tense. *I'm still here, you know.*

'She was pushed off a balcony, yeah?' He says, lighting up a fag like he couldn't care less.

Maddy nods slowly. 'It gave way.'

'What did?'

'The railing.'

'Ah right, gotcha, was it like an accident then?'

She pulls a face. 'In a way … if you believe in accidents.'

'Did he mean to kill her though? You must know – had his eyes gone? Did you see the red mist?'

'She messed him around.'

'Was she cheatin'?'

'She was flirting around his friend, Aaron.'

'But did she cheat though?'

'I think Gabriel had his suspicions.'

'And he just lost it?'

*That is such a lie. Why are you lying?*

They're standing in front of me. He's smoking, while she casually kicks at the bench with her pristine Air Max trainers.

*Gabe loved me*, I say. *He still does, I know it. You were the jealous one, but he'd never have gone for you. Gabe loves me.*

Maddy's expression hardens, changing instantly from plain to gargoyle.

My heart pumps and I step back with my arms up to protect myself, only of course I don't in any real sense. But the phantom instinctive response makes me realise that I know that look. I've seen it before.

The full moon lights up a beautiful indigo sky while my mind crashes with a realisation as heavy and impossible to ignore as forked lightning underlined by thunder.

*It was you. You pushed me.*

I'm there again in that moment, tumbling through the air in seconds that stretch with hopelessness and inevitability before I once again smack head first onto concrete.

*You killed me*, I say, all calm and matter of fact. And I don't know if we really are communicating, but Maddy's frown deepens, her mouth twisted and sneery.

*Did you mean to kill me?*

Maddy looks away abruptly, staring towards the beech tree.

*I mean you looked angry at the time, but it was the railing, wasn't it?*

Again, there's a brief flash of white as she kicks at the bench.

'Hey, what you doin'? That's disrespectful,' the lad says.

'She's a bitch.'

'I thought you were friends. What's your beef?'

'She wasn't a good friend. It was one-sided. She let me down all the time.'

'What you sayin'?'

She looks me over, her eyes as cold as a crocodile's. 'She didn't know anyone when she came to London. I introduced her to everyone. I did so much for her.'

'And your point is?' He takes a long drag on his cigarette and flicks ash on the ground. 'You've lost me?'

'She didn't appreciate those who loved her. She took the piss.'

'Her boyfriend – he did it, yeah?'

Maddy's eyes narrow to slits, and her mouth is a mean, thin slice through her face. 'I saw her fall – blood everywhere.'

'She die instantly?'

'She was still breathing in the helicopter, unconscious though.'

'You were with her?'

'I held her hand. She was breathing.'

*You're not a proper person*, I say. *You don't feel anything unless it's about you. You're not human in the true sense.*

The lad zips up his jacket. 'It's gone cold,' he says.

Maddy takes something out of her pocket and sits down.

'What are you doin'?'

She scratches at the plaque with a key, scoring through my

name. 'I was gonna write something,' she says, 'but I can't be arsed.'

He moves in next to her, puts his arm around her, and kisses her neck. She turns towards him, their mouths find each other, and their tongues loll together like trapped eels.

*How can you make out here?*

The lad pulls back. 'This is disrespectful. She was your mate.' He takes her stubby hand and pulls her over to Lionel's bench, pushing her down until she lies back, legs in the air. He moves in on top of her.

'Jakey.' She laughs. 'Behave.'

There's a cracking sound. He sits up. 'What was that?'

'Did you kick it? You must have done.' Maddy points at the seat of Lionel's bench where one of the slats has split.

'Jeez, I thought it was haunted for a minute. This bench is rotten.' He peers at Lionel's plaque. 'Look, how weird is that – this dude died today.'

'You what?'

'Look at the date, he died today, but years ago, obviously.'

'Let me see. So he did.'

'It's been here years, no wonder the wood's crackin' up.'

Maddy pokes the seat of Lionel's bench where a piece of wood's splintered off. She pushes at it, making it crack again and part of it falls away.

*Don't do that*, I shout.

'Get up a minute, Jakey.' Maddy stands back and then kicks at Lionel.

*Stop it*, I shout. *Stop.*

*Lionel, are you OK?* I have no idea what he can or can't feel.

There's a louder crack as Maddy's shoe breaks through one of the slats of Lionel's bench. She laughs. 'Help, my foot's gone through.'

'You psycho.' He helps her out. 'There aren't any cameras, are there?'

They both look around and up towards the nearest lamp posts.

She shrugs. 'Looks OK.'

*Are you all right, Lionel? I know you don't speak at night, but just this once please say something and let me know you're OK?*

Jakey hugs himself. 'It's cold, babe. Are your parents out?'

'Yeah, we can party at mine,' she says, and he grabs her arse, as she looks back at the bench with a twisted, triumphant half-smile.

All is quiet, all is still, and the bench that is Lionel remains bolted upright even though its seat has collapsed and is broken at one end.

*Lionel? Please speak to me.*

The river flows, the lamplight reflected in the water showing it to be calm.

*Lionel, I'm so worried about you.*

What will I do if he's no longer here? How will I cope? One friend is enough; I know that now – please, let me have that.

There is no more reliving to do. I am well and truly trapped in the living death that is my reality and the night is long, longer than ever, as I wait, willing Lionel to be fine, but aware I won't know for sure until sunrise.

A rat's tail flickers within the reeds. And a police siren sounds.

People walk past after the pubs close and there are cyclists and dog walkers and the occasional lovers. And I hate them for holding hands in front of me. Don't they realise how hurtful that is for lovers forced apart?

I search the sky for stars but there are none.

*Oh, Lionel.*

The sun rises shrouded in fog.

*Lionel, good morning. How are you? I've been worrying about you all night. Are you OK? Please say something.*

The fog has enveloped us. The river's hidden and only the ground immediately ahead is visible.

*Lionel, I don't know if you realise but it's morning. The sun is up, somewhere behind all this fog. Sorry, I don't mean to disturb you, but I have to know you're OK – please just say one word, anything will do – swear at me if you like. I won't mind. Are you OK? Please tell me you are.*

I wait and watch and listen and hope.

People pass and dogs pause, but I barely notice.

The longest morning follows the longest night until eventually the fog lifts and sunlight breaks through.

The warmth reaches me. I can feel it. I really can.

*Lionel, look at that sunshine, you love days like this.*

The warmth penetrates my wood, but now even the sun proves irritating, as it merely serves to underline how much I have lost.

Two days later a truck draws up and two workmen, one young, one old, and dressed in yellow high-visibility vests get out and from the back they unload tools and machinery. The young one with the tattoo of a snake encircling his arm works nearest me to unscrew the bolts that have held Lionel in place for over twenty years, while his workmate with the swallow tattoo takes care of the opposite end.

'I'll just grab those slats.' The young one pulls at the broken wood until they come lose and he bungs them in the back of the truck. They then work together to dismantle what's left, and with one at either end they lift the remaining bulk of Lionel's bench and place it in the back of the truck.

# THIRTY-FOUR

Lionel has gone. In his place remain only the concrete paving slabs onto which he was once bolted. And to think he went on his death day – who would have thought the same thing could happen twice on the same date?

The days are long, longer than ever, and the nights much the same. The one and only positive thing I can do is to keep trying to break through.

Everyone that sits on this bench by the beech tree hears something of my story, even if it is only the final scream. That always gets them. Perhaps it's the frequency, my hysterical pitch, that ensures that even the least aware hears it. They always move.

'Don't like it here,' a girl with pink streaks in her hair says, after happily munching her boyfriend's face off for half an hour.

'What's up?' he says.

'Got this really odd feeling. I don't like it. Let's go.'

*I am here. I exist (sort of), and I do feel. Sadly, I continue to feel.*

Susannah brings the dogs. She comes most days as part of her fitness routine. Always she slows as she approaches and shoos the dogs away, although they piss on me anyway as soon as she sits and closes her eyes to think, pray, meditate or whatever it is she does.

*Susannah.* I always talk to her, but for all her yoga and meditation mumbo jumbo she's not tuned in. Beyond a slight chill, she senses nothing, not like Alicia who gets me, but it frightens her and rather than act and help she blocks it out and avoids me.

Susannah pats the seat. 'See you tomorrow,' she says, and leans over to straighten the bear that's now blackened by rain and mould.

*Susannah, please bring Alicia to visit. It's ages since I've seen my little sis. Is she refusing to come or something?*

The dogs bark. They're barking at me of course, though Susannah's oblivious.

'Boys – shush.' She rounds them up and walks towards home.

A group of lady walkers march past, their arms swinging high and low to show they're serious about their walking. A mother chases her small boy who wants to walk with anyone but her, and a couple of pregnant women waddle by as if their babies are already engaged, head down, ready to squeeze out in the slowest, most difficult dive.

Funny, that reminds me of how I left the living world head first, the crucial difference being – I was pushed. *Was Lionel ready to leave the second time around?* I miss him so much, but I guess he was happy to go, judging by the way he vanished without a word. But then again, that's what most people do, only they do it just the once.

I think of him all day, while by night it's Gabe. I can't sleep. I don't rest. There is no peace.

'This is it, that's the one, on the left there.' A man riding a red mobility trike points at the bench as he motors towards it.

'Are you sure?' his friend says. 'It's not how I remember it.'

'I never forget a place.' He parks up beside me. 'Look, there's that grand old beech tree and the weeping willows opposite – remember?'

'Oh yeah, the weeping willows – I didn't realise there were loads of flats opposite though. I didn't really notice those before.'

'Maybe your mind edited out the ugliness.'

'Yes, I do that – makes life easier.' He laughs. 'That's definitely the plaque, I remember that.'

'Read it out, Phil, I've forgotten my glasses.'

'Hold on, it's a bit scratched – honestly who would do such a thing? I can still read it: "Lauren Bethany Miller 1995–2012. As we love her, so we miss her".'

'Aw, that's sweet, isn't it? She was loved, is loved – never forgotten, that's the main thing,' the man on the mobility scooter says. 'Are you there, Lauren love? My name's Mikey, you tried to reach me a few weeks back but it wasn't a good time for me. I wasn't feeling well and that meant I wasn't prepared to listen and I apologise for that. But I'm in a better place right now and that's why we've come back. I feel I'm able to help if you're still willing to come through.' He closes his eyes.

White petals blow on the breeze and decorate the path like sugar sprinkles, while geese fly above and sunshine makes the brown river glisten like gold.

I take the deepest non-breath breath. *Hello, Mikey, thanks so much for coming back. It's Lauren here as it says on the plaque, but call me Ren. That's what all my friends call me.*

I tell him everything. It's all come back to me: the party, the conflict with Gabe caused by my comedy twerking with Aaron, and the unmasking of Maddy, and how I thought she was jealous of what I had with Gabe and yet that wasn't quite it.

Jamil and his mates came by as I tried to sober up on the balcony. They looked me over as they went past. One of them said, 'Yeah, I would,' and the others laughed. They knocked on the door, and I imagined fights, knives, emergency calls to the police. Gabe answered and told them they weren't welcome. I held my breath, fearing the worst.

Jamil sneered and said, 'I know where you live, bruv.' And Gabe squared up to him, told him how he knew about his business, who he used, where he "works", and that it would be a shame if that knowledge had to be shared.

'Party's breaking up, anyhow,' Gabe said, and I don't know if his words worked, or if it was the fact Jamil took a call with a better offer, but they backed out and the panic was over. Gabe was the hero. The music was turned up and everyone jumped up to Skrillex. I danced for a while, and then peeled away and went back outside. Maddy followed, passing me a plastic water bottle full of vodka and lemonade. 'Are we good?' she said, and I shrugged and told her there was obviously some sort of problem and that I didn't get what it was about.

She instantly launched into a tirade, listing all the ways I'd let her down during the three months we'd known each other. She'd done everything for me, she said, introduced me to everyone and yet how did I repay her? In her mind, I'd ditched her for Gabriel. She could cite each and every time, every meetup after college that I'd called off, every evening I said I had work to do, every potential night out where she thought I'd chosen Gabe over her.

'It wasn't like that,' I told her. 'One time I was ill and another I had too much work on and Susannah wouldn't let me out at one point.'

She was shouting, furious, I had so let her down. I shrugged and apologised and told her it was never intentional. 'Where do we go from here?' I asked, and she told me I had to be more considerate and think of her feelings.

'I love you,' she said, 'I just want to be with you.' And I laughed, incredulous, confused even. What does that mean? What is she saying? Because it didn't feel like love. It was more like an attack and an attempt to seize back control.

Gabe came out to join us on the balcony and looked at me quizzically, like he didn't get what was going on. And you know how sometimes you laugh when you shouldn't, and because you know you shouldn't, it makes it worse and you can't stop.

Perhaps it was a nervous reaction, I don't know, but me laughing certainly annoyed Maddy and it was as if it came from nowhere when she reacted in an impulsive and petulant way with a frustrated and forceful almighty shove, determined to wipe the smile off my face.

# THIRTY-FIVE

Another bright morning follows the previous five and I've grown used to the warmth and how it penetrates the wood of the bench making me feel positive and almost alive. And so when it becomes particularly warm I assume it's simply the sun, until I hear a gasp and a voice I recognise.

It's Mum and she's rushing towards me with a bouquet in her hand. She's wearing a beige shift dress and jacket – an outfit I've not seen before – and I'm glad to see she's dropped the mourning dress. Black was always my colour.

'Look how faded it is already,' she says, as she places the cellophane-wrapped flowers on the bench beside the mouldy bear.

She has a face on her. Reminds me of that game, Sweet and Sour – definitely sour. 'Someone's scratched this.' Her hot breath wets the plaque. 'It's been vandalised, look.'

'You're kidding?' Jay inspects the damaged metal.

'That'll be some idiot who doesn't know any better,' Billy tuts.

'Can we do anything about it?' Mum asks.

'It's not very deep,' Billy says. 'It can probably be fixed.'

'Whatever next?' Mum sits down, as do Jay and Billy, facing the river. They appear blank-eyed with straight mouths as they try to hold it together.

'Bear's had it.' Jay holds up the blackened bear.

'Leave it,' Mum says, like she thinks it's some sort of good luck charm that should never be moved.

*Mum, really, dump it – it's gross.*

Mum sighs. 'Ren was born on a day like this. My spring lamb – that's what I called her when she was small.' She takes a tissue from her bag. 'It all goes by in a flash. She couldn't wait to be eighteen. Do you remember?' Mum smiles. 'Her eighteenth was going to be better than anyone else's.'

'Probably would have been,' Jay says. 'She wanted a pool party at her dad's house – would have been classic.'

'Yeah, if they let her have it there,' Billy says – ever the pessimist.

'I don't see why not,' Mum says. 'Pass me that bag, Jay.' He does as she asks and she retrieves a cake tin. She's only gone and baked me a cake.

Billy says, 'That's one hell of a cake.' It's white with purple lettering that spells 'REN' in a love heart. Mum slices three wedges of cake.

'We're not singing happy birthday,' Mum says. 'That'll really set me off.'

Billy nods and bites into his cake.

'That's good cake, Mum,' Jay says, 'but I've not got much appetite.' He puts his piece back in the tin, while Billy opens a plastic carrier bag and offers Mum and Jay a can each.

Jay smiles. 'You bought "K" – the stuff Ren liked.'

'It is her eighteenth,' Billy says.

'Her first legal drink,' Mum says.

'She'd been drinking for ages.' Jay makes a toast, 'To Ren.' And they clink cans and knock back the cider even though it's got to be morning and Mum never drinks during the day.

'Happy birthday, my darling girl, I wish you were here with us.' Mum crushes the empty cider can in her hands and I catch sight of her wrist. She has a tattoo: a tiny ultramarine dragonfly with four delicate wings and three curly letters underneath that spell "Ren".

*Oh, Mum, what have you done? That's going to look terrible when you're old. You'll regret that, everyone does.*

*Anyway, more to the point, if you really want to make my day, how about an update on Gabriel – what's going on? Has Mikey explained everything to the police? Is he out and on his way to see me?*

Both Jay and Billy put an arm around Mum, who sits between them looking older than I remember. 'I'm going to talk to Nicholas about fixing the plaque,' she says. 'How could someone do that? It's disgraceful. Do you think it was a friend of that Gabriel Walker?'

'It could have been anyone, Mum.'

'He's bound to be part of a gang,' Billy says.

'We should report it,' Jay says. 'There might be CCTV footage.'

Mum sighs and wipes her eyes. 'I want to go now.'

*Thanks for coming, so nice to see you, but I wish you'd brought good news.*

Later, long after Mum, Jay and Billy have gone, Alicia arrives, holding a fancy bunch of flowers in a box-shaped bag. She pauses before she reaches me.

'Why have you stopped?' Susannah asks. 'Come and organise the flowers.'

'Why didn't you get black ones?'

'The white ones are so pretty, don't you think?'

Alicia fusses over the box of white lilies, rearranging them slightly before placing them next to Mum's bouquet and the rotting bear. 'Happy birthday, Ren.'

Dad follows up behind pushing a wheelchair. *Who is that?*

Only one person I know has such a perfect hairdo – Judy, his mother, my grandmother, the aged ballerina, but she looks different, like her face has collapsed on one side. And her left eye is half-closed, the eyelid all droopy. She's had a stroke – so much for the health benefits of living in Chelsea. And she's holding a bear. *Not another one.*

Nicholas parks the wheelchair next to the bench and secures its brake.

'Shall we put the bear by the flowers, Mummy?' He takes the

bear from Judy's limp hand and places it next to the old mouldy one, and sits down next to Susannah and Alicia to watch the river just as Mum, Jay and Billy had earlier.

*Hi, guys, good to see you – it's been a while. And, especially pleased to see my little sis – looking good, Al. Nice to see you as well, Grandma Judy and sorry if you're not too well right now. Anyway, listen up, I have to see Gabriel. Is he out? I have to know. He matters more than anything.*

Alicia freezes as if she senses danger. 'Can we go now?' she says.

'We've only just got here, sweetie,' Susannah says.

'It's just too hard. I miss Ren so much.'

'I know you do, darling,' Susannah says.

Alicia shakes her head, and says, 'When I'm here, it's like I can still hear her and it upsets me – those things she says.'

Nicholas looks askance. 'Sorry, what's that?'

'It's like I can hear Ren, but I don't know if it's just my imagination?'

'I imagine I hear her voice sometimes,' Susannah says. 'I'm sure we all do.'

'You don't understand. I can't be here,' Alicia says.

'I know it's tough, honey, but we need to stay a little while longer.'

Dad's jaw tenses, and his fists are clenched. 'She didn't even make eighteen. It's not right. Thank God the police have charged someone.'

*I want an update? Where are we at, have you guys realised yet that the police have the wrong person? Is Gabe out?*

Why doesn't anyone listen to me? Every time, Alicia just looks completely spooked and what help is that?

*Lionel, what should I do?* Momentarily, I forget that he's gone.

Alicia stands stock-still in front and stares, her head cocked to one side as if she's listening.

*Alicia, I'm here, it's me.*

She steps aside and runs to the dogs as if they need her.

*Alicia,* I shout, *it's me that needs you not them.*

Late evening, my worst fears are confirmed as who should rock up alongside Carina and Idris, but that jealous, possessive, controlling lunatic Maddy.

*I don't get it, how is she still out walking the streets like a sane, law-abiding citizen? Did no one listen to Mikey? Or worse, did he not bother to pass on the information?*

*The wood of this bench is the worst prison. The warmth of the sun no consolation for all that I've lost. Mikey was my last and only hope.*

'Hey, Ren-Ren, happy birthday.' Carina strokes the back of the bench and sits down, while Maddy parks her fat arse next to her and Idris remains standing.

'Come on, sit down,' Carina says.

'Nah, don't want to.'

'Why not?'

'Dunno, doesn't feel right.' Carina pulls him down next to her and he passes around some cans of lager.

Carina makes a toast. 'Happy birthday, lovely, beautiful Ren.'

'To Ren,' Idris says, 'loved your singing and you were all right – miss yer.'

'Ren,' is all Maddy says, as she raises her can a fraction.

'Trial's coming up?' Idris says.

'Next week,' Maddy says.

'You ready for it?' Idris asks.

She shrugs. 'I've never been a witness before. I'm told it can be daunting.'

'How long will it last?' Carina asks.

'Two to three weeks,' Maddy says.

Carina shakes her head. 'I still can't believe it. I mean, I just never thought Gabriel was like that.'

'What about the twisted ankle?' Maddy says. 'That wasn't an

accident – Gabriel caused it somehow. It'll come up at the trial I bet.'

I will the earth to crack open and swallow her whole, envisioning a furious shake from the deep that causes the ground to quake and crack, throwing my true friends out and away to safety while taking Maddy down, and yet she remains safe and upright and as popular as ever. Why can no one see?

'I can't sit here,' Idris says. 'It feels wrong.'

*That's right, Idris. It's all wrong – Gabe banged up for something he didn't do.* And it's there again, that moment when I'm out on the balcony, outside Aaron's front door, something is said and it's so absurd – like she's in love with me – as if I mean everything to her.

I laugh, I laugh too much, and she lashes out, sending me reeling and crashing back, where I topple and double up over the balcony railing that's not as safe as it should be. It gives way. I'm going down, falling through air, as the hard, unforgiving ground rushes up to meet me.

# THIRTY-SIX

Gabe: how he hugged me, held me, kissed me and everything stopped, the world fell away – nothing else mattered. This is what I have – beautiful moments that I relive endlessly in the hope and belief my constant thoughts will call him to me.

Any hint of warmth raises my hopes: *Is it Gabe?*

No, it's my family, as in the original one that never quite was: Mum, Nicholas and Jay.

Mum looks terrible, her eyes puffy and her mouth downturned, although she's dressed in her smart stuff: a navy skirt suit with scarf. Jay has his arm around her, and Nicholas is by her other side, talking quietly, his expression concerned. 'I've got someone to fix the plaque,' he says. 'They're coming next week.' Mum nods.

'Here, have a seat, Mum.' Jay guides her to the bench. She sits down and Dad and Jay sit either side. She bursts into tears.

'What sort of world is this? I don't understand.'

'I'm livid,' Jay says.

'People can be tried twice, there is that possibility,' Dad says, 'if we can just uncover new evidence.'

*What is it? Is Gabriel free?*

'He did it. I know he did it,' Mum says.

*Hold on. What about Mikey? You know, the guy with the red mobility trike? Didn't he explain it all to you and the police? I told him everything: like how it was Maddy and that the little kid two doors down from Aaron's flat could prove it all.*

'And as for that psychic freak in the wheelchair…' Mum

frowns, her forehead like lined paper. 'Some people will say anything to get attention.'

'The truth will come out one day,' Jay says.

'The police aren't looking for anyone else,' Dad says. 'That's telling.'

'But how could the jury believe him?' Mum says. 'He looked as guilty as sin. Why couldn't they see that?'

'Juries convict on the strength of the evidence,' Dad says. 'It wasn't strong enough. The police did say cases like this are notoriously hard to prove.'

Mum is in floods of tears. Jay puts his arm around her and Dad reaches over to hold her hand.

'I'm gonna walk for a bit, clear my head,' Jay says. He gets up and walks towards the bridge.

Mum looks up, turning towards Dad, and they hug.

That's weird, I think, after all these years.

'She was my baby,' Mum says.

Dad nods. 'She was a great kid,' he says. 'She would have done great things. You did a fantastic job.'

'I feel like I failed her,' Mum says.

'You're a brilliant mum,' Dad says. 'If anyone failed her, it was me.'

Mum shakes her head. 'We were too young.'

Dad nods. 'And I was too single-minded. I couldn't see beyond my career. I didn't do the right thing by you.'

'It wouldn't have worked.' Mum laughs. 'Be honest, you weren't into me.'

*Great to reminisce, guys. And I know I said I was interested in the past and why it didn't work out, but more to the point, Gabe's out? He's free? Mum, Dad, you've made my day and all days forever more. I told you it wasn't him. Does he know where I am? Have you told him? Please tell him, he has to know. I love him so much.*

# THIRTY-SEVEN

Lionel, there are so many questions I wish I could ask you. I thought we had forever. It's the mistake we all make. You said we all need to know what questions to ask, but what good is it if they come too late? Every day now I think of questions I'd like to ask: What made you scared? When were you happiest? Was there anything you wish you'd known when you were seventeen? Where exactly was your bakery? And what was the most popular cake? Some answers I can guess, but it's the detail I'll never get.

You once said that you thought I trod lightly on the earth, causing no harm. That's all that matters, isn't it, to be kind? Well, you were kind to me – always.

These days the living annoy me with their active ways – walking up whenever and staying as long as they like without even a thank you. I am a grumpy old grouch already, prematurely aged with the discolouration of my wood – seventeen/eighteen going on eighty, I reckon, or at least trombones.

Where are the workmen with their high-visibility vests and tattooed arms? I thought they'd have been back by now with a replacement bench. Not that Lionel is replaceable. Funny, if you'd asked me a few months back I'd have said I want someone young, someone I can relate to and have a laugh with, but to be honest I can't wish an early death on anyone, not even the Lunatic. It's not in me to feel like that, so I don't mind if the replacement bench is dedicated to someone who's a hundred years old because I'm sure we'll get on. We'll have to…

'This is it, just up here,' someone says. It's a young man's voice – familiar.

Heat engulfs me, but it's welcome warmth as if I'm by an open fire having recently returned from a freezing winter boat trip.

I look up at the sun, but that's not it.

'That's weird that the bench is here,' a young male voice says. 'This is the way I used to walk Ren home.'

*I can't believe it.*

*At last* – the Etta James song blasts in my head, as my phantom eyes fill with tears of joy. Gabriel's here in front of me – dressed in a white T-shirt and jeans. He's tall, lean and the hottest guy I've seen since the last time I saw him.

Am I imagining this?

*Gabe, is that really you?*

I'm out of the bench, flying to him, jumping into his arms – wrapping my legs around him. *Gabriel, I don't believe it.* I kiss him. *Kiss me.*

Why doesn't he?

Aaron hangs back to allow Gabe to get a good look.

I'm a greying, weathered bench – that's all.

*Gabe, think of what I was, not what I have become.*

Gabe reads the plaque and shakes his head. 'Lauren – what's that all about? She hated that name. I used to say it sometimes to wind her up and she'd punch me every time. That bit's good though – "As we love her, so we miss her". That's true, I like that.' He bites his lip, and looks down.

Aaron puts an arm around Gabe's shoulders. 'Mate, you've been through so much. I never doubted you, none of us did. We all knew it weren't you and we kept saying it, even at the memorial service. It was so frustrating – no one would listen.'

'I wish her family thought the same as you.'

'The jury believed you – that's what matters. And what about that psychic bloke – didn't he provide fresh evidence?'

'He said he stopped here by the bench, and Ren told him firstly that she's called Ren and secondly that it was Maddy. And he said that she told him that there was a little curly-haired boy who lives two doors down from you and that the kid could corroborate it. Trouble is the police weren't interested. Apparently they're always hearing from nutters and besides as far as they were concerned, the Crown Prosecution Service's case was rock solid.'

'But they looked for the boy, yeah?'

'Apparently so, but who knows? My dad reckons they probably didn't bother because I'm black.'

Aaron nods. 'I can believe that.'

'Who does live two doors down from you?'

'There's new people now. My mum says that around that time there were about fifteen illegal immigrants squashed into that two-bed flat. The tenant was subletting.'

'Where were they from?'

'Somalia, I think – that's where the new lot are from anyhow.'

'Did you ever see a little boy though?'

'To be honest I didn't, but then some of them never left the flat. Saying that, my mum was chatting to one of the women the other day and she's going to see what she can do. She said a friend of a friend of a friend might know where they are, but then again is anyone going to listen to a little kid?'

'You never know, they might do. It's worth a go. People need to know the truth.'

'The thing is, that psychic bloke – he knew she was called Ren. How could he know that?' Gabe looks back at the plaque.

*Because I told him, Gabe – Mikey can hear me. Can you hear me?*

Gabriel looks away and squints at the river – the sunlight so strong it's turned the water to a shimmering sheet of gold. 'Aaron, mate,' he says, his face serious, 'I need to be on my own for a while.'

'Mate, totally understand. D'you want me to wait for you?'

'Nah, you're all right.'

'I'll head to Fenton's. Join us there if you're up to it.'

'Thanks, mate.' They come together in a brief hug and as they do so I too feel Gabriel's fine, lean torso and his thin but muscular arms as if they're around me.

'Take care, mate,' Aaron says. 'Message me, yeah?'

'I'll call you.'

Gabriel sits down and his fingers curl around the edge of the bench's seat.

I concentrate on the small, slight warmth from his palms and fingertips and it travels right into me to my very centre where my phantom heart beats.

*Gabe, you have no idea how I've longed for this.*

'Hey, Ren,'

*Can you hear me?*

'How's my girl?'

*At last you're here and you can hear me.*

Gabe's shoulders twitch involuntarily as if a shiver's passed over him. 'All the time I was locked up I dreamt of being here by the river with you,' he says.

*Gabe, I've been longing for you – to see you, to hear you, to know you're all right – I've missed you so much.*

'I'm going to get up in a minute and jump those benches again, like I did before. That was a laugh. D'you remember?'

*I remember everything.*

'I'm going to jump them and go flying like I did before. Did you realise I faked it? I didn't really fall. I jumped and lay flat because I knew you'd come running and that I could pull you down and kiss you and hold you and never let go. I should never have let you go. If I'd just grabbed hold of you that night on the balcony…'

*Don't blame yourself. That's crazy. You weren't to know. It all happened so fast. She flipped.*

'We were good together. No one can take that away, whatever they say…'

Warmth permeates the entire bench, as he looks back at the plaque.

*You look worried, don't be, everything's OK now.*

He gets out his phone and points it at the code that opens the Ren Miller Memorial website. Here we go again with the embarrassing photos: me as a fat baby with a tuft of dark hair, me as a toddler with ice cream all over my face, aged about four swimming with armbands and rubber ring, and then at ten with Jay on holiday in Cornwall, and a year later in Brittany, at sixteen I'm on top of Haytor with Kemi and we're wearing badger hats, and then at seventeen it's Westfield with Carina and the Lunatic. And then I'm by the lake at Ambrose House with Alicia, Dad, Susannah and the stupid dogs and finally around the table at home, Cherry Tree Close, with Mum and Jay – Billy took that. It's enough to make anyone cry but it doesn't stop there. Here comes the singing. There I am in that black lace dress, hair pinned up, thick black eyeliner, as, eyes closed, I sing Amy Winehouse's *You Know I'm No Good.*

*That was the night we got together, Holly's party – my first proper gig.*

A tear falls onto the screen of Gabe's phone.

*You were so lovely to me that night.*

He's shaking as he watches, blinking as tears fall into his lap.

*Gabe, you don't have to watch this.*

He continues to listen as Mum goes on about the great void that's opened up in her life, and there's Susannah, Kemi, Carina and even the Lunatic lying about how much she loved me.

Gabe turns it off.

*Phew – can't stand listening to her. What a bitch, even though I don't think she meant to do exactly what she did, the outcome is the same.*

He sits forward, his face in his hands.

'She ruined everything,' he says. 'She went psycho, and yeah, I get that maybe she didn't mean it to turn out how it did. I mean nine times out of ten that shove probably would have come to nothing, only the railing gave way. Why can't she admit that?'

*It's done now.*

'We should have had forever.'

*We do in a way. All's good now you're here. Your freedom frees me somehow.*

The top of his head looks so soft with those thick dark curls. I wish I could touch his hair and kiss the warmth of him: his neck, face and lips.

His shoulders shake. He looks up, his eyes watery, as he squints at the sun.

*You sense me, I know it – what's my favourite song?*

He stares into the distance towards the weeping willows. And I wish the wood of my bench would disintegrate to dust and let me out.

Gabe stands up facing the river and somehow facing me.

His beautiful light hazel eyes with the little dark flecks are all watery as he looks into me and I drink up their warmth and wonder.

*I love you.*

There's a slight flicker of movement on his lips as he goes to speak but stops and shakes his head in a move so small it's imperceptible to all but me.

*It's me, Gabe. I'm here for you.*

'Ren?'

*You called out to me. I couldn't leave.*

'Ren, are you really here? It doesn't make sense. I don't believe in things like that, but then again I keep thinking of that time we went to Camden Square to look at Amy Winehouse's house and you said then that you thought something of her must be there in the air.'

*It's me. I'm here.*

Gabe's eyes widen and again he wells up. 'You're so beautiful.'

I smile and look into his soft, kind eyes.

'I'm going to come here every day,' he says. 'This is our place, somewhere I can be close to you. I'm going to come all the time.'

A second stretches to seem never-ending as Gabe's eyes take me in.

'I love you.' He sits back down like he's been knocked back onto the bench.

*I love you.*

*Ren and Gabe forever.*

'I'll never forget you,' he says.

*I will always be with you, Gabe, loving you, willing you on to do good things with good people.*

*Promise you'll make the most of each and every moment.*

He nods, and the tears filling his eyes begin to fall.

'I love you.' He says it with me, and we are one and the same watching the river shimmer like a sheet of gold so bright and brilliant that we cannot look for long.

## Slang Definitions

- **amazeballs:** extremely good or impressive; amazing
- **banging:** great, excellent
- **bare:** very, a lot of
- **beef:** complain, to have a grudge
- **bro:** short for brother, or a male friend
- **butters:** ugly
- **chatting shit:** talking rubbish
- **dank:** used to describe something of high quality, something that's good
- **dead** (session)**:** rubbish (party)
- **deep:** difficult to understand, or very intense or profound
- **do one:** slang for telling someone to "get lost"
- **endz:** your zone, your streets, your area
- **fit:** hot, extremely good-looking
- **hood:** an area where someone lives, the ghetto.
- **innit:** contraction of "isn't it", or a general positive exclamation meaning "yes, i agree"
- **jump your bones:** to have sexual intercourse
- **that's out:** when someone says something stupid or something that's not right
- **piff:** superior to the average, or attractive
- **sick:** crazy, cool, insane, good
- **soz**: sorry
- **wicked**: cool, great

## Acknowledgements

Thank you to my editor Monica Byles whose knowledge and precision made the editing process an enjoyable experience.

Natalia Jefferson and Serena Huddle provided early insights that helped improve the script, as did Erzsi Deak. A big thank you to the Southbank set: David Bausor, Christabel Cooper, Kyo Choi, Dominique Jackson, EJ Swift and Colin Tucker who were there from the start.

My daughters, Zanzi and Bijou, helped with the latest slang. And thanks to my partner Daryl, and my mum and dad for their encouragement and support.

DATE DUE

| | |
|---|---|
| | |
| | |
| | |
| | |
| | |
| | |
| | |
| | |
| | |
| | |
| | |
| | |
| | |
| | |
| | |
| | |
| | |
| | |

PRINTED IN U.S.A.

CPSIA information can be obtained
at www.ICGtesting.com
Printed in the USA
BVOW09s1018200817
492483BV00012B/24/P